'Yo... Nor am... 'Not for... ng or beep or spontaneously combust.'

... hours?' They were going to be out *that* long?

... okay?'

... guess.' It was better than staying the night, right?

... to cave loses.'

... oses what?'

... s sudden unexpected smile was too wicked for her ...ing.

...Vhat you should be asking is what the winner receives.'

...ephanie turned in her seat, her heart drumming heavy-...etal style. 'What do you win if I cave?'

... taste.'

...)f…?'

'What do you think?' he asked, too softly.

...Ay blog is ready to be bought but *I'm* not on the table, ...r Wolfe,' she breathed, trying to be icy. And failing.

...Not yet—and it's Jack.'

Not *ever*, Mr Wolfe.'

You're afraid I'll bite? I won't. I'm talking about one ...iss.'

...he stared at him. He was driving along as if he *hadn't* ... care in the world. As if he *hadn't* just suggested ...omething wildly inappropriate. And so wildly tempting.

...inally he glanced over at her. 'You can't tell me you haven't considered the idea already.'

**Natalie Anderson** adores a happy ending—which is why she always reads the back of a book first. Just to be sure. So you can be sure you've got a happy ending in your hands right now—because she promises nothing less. Along with happy endings she loves peppermint-filled dark chocolate, pineapple juice and extremely long showers. Not to mention spending hours teasing her imaginary friends with dating dilemmas. She tends to torment them before eventually relenting and offering—you guessed it—a happy ending. She lives in Christchurch, New Zealand, with her gorgeous husband and four fabulous children.

If, like her, you love a happy ending, be sure to come and say hi on facebook/authornataliea, on Twitter @authornataliea, or at her website/blog: www.natalie-anderson.com

### Books by Natalie Anderson

*Whose Bed Is It Anyway?*
*The Right Mr Wrong*
*Blame It on the Bikini*
*Waking Up in the Wrong Bed*
*First Time Lucky?*

**Visit the author profile page at
millsandboon.co.uk for more titles**

# TYCOON'S TERMS OF ENGAGEMENT

BY
NATALIE ANDERSON

Published in Great Britain 2015
by Mills & Boon, an imprint of Harlequin (UK) Limited,
Eton House, 18-24 Paradise Road, Richmond, Surrey, TW9 1SR

© 2015 Natalie Anderson

ISBN: 978-0-263-24882-1

Harlequin (UK) Limited's policy is to use papers that are natural,
renewable and recyclable products and made from wood grown in
sustainable forests. The logging and manufacturing processes conform
to the legal environmental regulations of the country of origin.

Printed and bound in Spain
by CPI, Barcelona

# TYCOON'S TERMS OF ENGAGEMENT

# CHAPTER ONE

'YOU'RE NOT TO leave me alone with him, you understand?' Stephanie Johnson—Steffi Leigh to her quadrillion blog subscribers—closed the passenger door and glared at her best friend.

'Stop stressing. It's not like he's dangerous.' Tara rummaged in her oversized handbag as she walked round to the footpath, not bothering to look up or to lock the car.

'He's more than dangerous. He's like God,' Stephanie argued. Because Jack Wolfe held her whole world in his hands. 'And you know I can't keep the act up for long.'

Long enough for the ninety-second vlogs she recorded in the corner of her bedroom—sure. But staying as 'Steffi Leigh' for a three-hour meeting out in the real world? She hadn't a hope. At least not without help.

Absently she nibbled on her fingernail, only to get a bite of fabric. *Ugh.* She'd forgotten she was wearing sleek white gloves—their purpose to hide the chewed-to-the-quick ugliness of her nails. Her whole vintage look was to hide her real, slightly screwed-up self.

'Well, if you'd stop rubbing your face…' Tara stepped in close, her blusher brush raised like the weapon it was. 'And stand still…'

As if that was possible. Her kitten-heeled shoes were half killing her toes, her stomach was churning and she was freezing, despite the weather app on her phone reckoning it was thirty-two degrees already. Stephanie waved Tara's annoying brush away and checked the time on her phone again.

'Let's go. We can't be late.' She didn't need the blusher—she'd probably turn beetroot the second he asked her a tricky question.

As she turned towards the hotel her panic sharpened. She was going to give herself away in the first five minutes... Because Steffi Leigh was all fiction. And Stephanie Johnson was a phony.

'Of *course* you can be late,' Tara scoffed, burrowing in her bag again. 'You're Steffi Leigh. You're going to make an entrance.'

Stephanie winced. That was going to happen anyway, given she looked as if she'd just stepped out of a nineteen-fifties sewing catalogue—all full-skirted dress, nipped-in waist, kid gloves, kitten heels and pin-curled hair. She could see people driving past and turning their heads, probably wondering if it was a photo shoot—what with the make-up artist touching up her face on the street.

If only she *was* a model. If only she wasn't going to have to speak and try to sell her site as some stellar investment.

'Stephanie.' Tara looked up and eyeballed her. 'You can do this. You need to.' Tara smiled. 'You've got to get on with your life.'

Stephanie looked at her friend and a fatalistic determination sank into her bones. Yeah, she could do this. Because she *had* to—not for her life, but her brother's.

She tucked her phone into her vintage bag, squared her shoulders and lifted her chin. She *was* Steffi Leigh, and today she'd do the best job of staying in character ever.

Fake it. Make it. *Rake* it in.

She walked the few yards to the grand columned entrance. The Raeburn Hotel was one of the oldest, and definitely the most glamorous of Melbourne's many five-star hotels, and the venue for her meeting with Jack Wolfe, CEO of the massive global media conglomerate that been publishing the world's most popular and trusted travel guides for years. His company had transitioned well into the on-line environment, and he was interested in talking to her about her blog.

*Monetising* had been a key word in the blogging/vlog-ging/have-your-own-channel world of the internet for years now. Anyone could start yapping online, but getting people to part with their cash to hear what you had to say…? That was the Holy Grail.

But right now an even better grail was within her grasp. Because it wasn't just a few followers wanting to pay her a couple of dollars a day, or funds from the few ads she could bear to have littering her design, it was a famous heir to a fortune offering a bundle of cash for the lot. And Stepha-nie was willing to do almost anything to get her hands on a decent amount of money. It was the only hope she had left to lift her brother out of his downward spiral. To get him into study, get his life started again.

A one-off instant cash offer would be incredible.

So Jack Wolfe could never know how much of a faker she was. That the huge platform she'd somehow accumu-lated was built on a façade that she projected from one corner of her small bedroom. If anyone ever saw the *rest* of the room…

The CEO of Wolfe Enterprises certainly wasn't going to. Jack Wolfe was getting nothing but the façade for a few hours. She had to get him to buy it. Literally.

She smiled as the liveried attendant held the door for her, then paused for a moment, trying not to blink in naive appreciation of the marble-columned lobby. It had been a while since she'd got out. And never had she spent much time in a place as opulent and expensive as this.

'I'm just nipping to the little girls' room,' Tara mur-mured.

'*Now?*'

'Your brother barricaded himself in the bathroom so I didn't get a chance to go before we left.' Tara shrugged.

Stephanie forgot the glorious surroundings and stared at Tara in horror. 'You didn't tell me that. Was he okay?' She'd thought Dan had been sleeping. Even now, months since his last operation, he needed his rest.

'He was *fine*. He was *sulking*.' Tara fossicked in her bag again, as if she'd dropped the Hope Diamond in there. 'Jeez, that boy knows how to play you.' She looked up and sent Steffi a disapproving look. 'Put the phone *away*. You don't need him emotionally manipulating you two seconds before this meeting.'

'He doesn't emotionally manipulate me.' Stephanie paused, her phone in her hand, embarrassed that Tara knew she'd been about to call and check up on him.

Tara shook her head and strode to the bathroom, barely watching where she was going, still searching for that elusive lost item in the bottom of her bag.

'He *doesn't*,' Stephanie muttered under her breath, and clicked her phone to check the time on the screen. And to make sure there were no messages from Dan.

There weren't.

She didn't know whether that fact ought to make her worry more.

But Tara had been right—now wasn't the time. Dan would have to wait a couple of hours. It was for *his* benefit that she was here. She'd head to the reception desk and get them to let Jack Wolfe know she'd arrived, and hopefully Tara would be back before he made it downstairs.

As she walked towards the beautifully clad reception staff she couldn't help noticing a lone man standing with his back to her at the far corner of the lounge area. Sleek leather briefcase in one hand, he was talking into his phone. His stance emanated strength...his attire denoted power. And his American accent carried across the clear space.

'I don't care if he's busy. I've waited long enough,' he snapped. 'Arrange it. Now.'

Turning, he stabbed his phone screen and then shoved it in his pocket.

Stephanie lifted her brows at the brusque arrogance of his demand. He was definitely used to giving orders, but he didn't do it nicely. Curious to see his face, she kept an eye on him as he turned towards the rest of the room. Dark-haired, tanned, ocean-blue eyes. He'd be attractive if all that anger wasn't radiating from his rigid posture.

He was looking down, but even so she could see the stark expression building in his eyes. Her footsteps faltered as she registered that he was feeling more than angry. He looked hurt. For a moment he looked utterly exposed, and the depth of his unhappiness stole her breath. A flood of sympathy rose unbidden, puckering her heart. For such a man to look so defeated, no matter how momentarily, it had to be something bad. And she understood bad. She knew heartache intimately.

He stiffened suddenly and looked up, across the short distance, right at *her*. Totally catching her gawping.

Instantly his expression changed. Closed. *Hardened*.

His blue eyes narrowed, focusing. And then to her astonishment he looked her over—slowly, blatantly—appraising every inch of her. All the way from her kitten-heeled feet to her perfectly curled hair.

Stephanie stood frozen, shocked, and just blinked back at him as he dared sum her up in one stare. His lips pressed into a thin line and his demeanour implied a total thumbs-down. He couldn't have looked less impressed—or more hostile.

Okay, so she wasn't *Top Model* striking, or *Cosmo* cover potential, but she wasn't bad. And with Tara having worked her magic she was more than passable. And even if she wasn't, his visual disapproval and dismissal was just plain rude.

Was he angry because he was embarrassed that she'd heard him? Or that she'd seen him looking upset for a second? She hadn't intended to eavesdrop—he'd been the one who hadn't had the courtesy even to try and refrain from letting the rest of the world hear his conversation.

Now she couldn't be sure she'd seen such bleakness in his eyes. And had she *really*, just for a moment, felt for him?

Well, she wasn't going to let him know he'd pierced her pride. Summoning every ounce of Steffi Leigh, she sent him her most sparkling smile—albeit insincere. Without waiting to see his reaction she turned her back on him and his wordless judgement and walked over to the receptionist.

'Could you please let Jack Wolfe know that Steffi Leigh is here to see him?'

'I'm Jack Wolfe.' A deep voice interrupted just behind her.

Stephanie's heart sank. But her already tense muscles braced even more. She'd known it—the accent had warned her. She just hadn't wanted to be right.

She smiled her thanks to the receptionist, but the woman wasn't paying her any attention—she was too busy making eyes at the man who'd spoken.

Yeah, he was like that—vacuuming up the sexual attention of every woman in the vicinity.

Quelling the nerves churning her stomach, Stephanie turned to face him.

The Wolfe Guides were geared towards the independent traveller. Those infinitely cool types who managed to travel around fifteen countries for nine months with only a small backpack on their backs and yet looked hip and stylish every step of the way. But Jack Wolfe wasn't in a quick-dry shirt. He wore a made-to-measure, made-to-perfection suit. And he definitely had to have chosen the shirt to complement his eyes and make their blue even more blindingly brilliant.

'You look exactly as you do in your blog profile, Ms Leigh.' He didn't make it sound as if it was a good thing.

So he'd recognised her and had *still* looked at her with such cold dismissal? *Nice.*

'Please call me Steffi,' she invited with crisp politeness, extending her hand. She'd start over. Pretend that intense moment had never happened. Ignore his rudeness.

'Not Steffi Leigh?' He took her hand in a firm grip.

'Just Steffi is fine.'

A pulse of energy shot into her fingers and up her arm, making her glad of the gloves. Because even through the cotton she could feel the warmth and strength of him and she couldn't tear her gaze from his. It had been too long since she'd looked such a handsome man in the eye. Okay, she'd never actually *seen* such a handsome man in real life before.

She'd never actually gone weak at the knees before either.

It was nerves, right? Or some Neanderthal woman instinct—to be drawn to the most powerful male in the room... She could use her brain better than this.

Tara had been wrong. This man *was* dangerous.

'Is Steffi short for Stephanie?' he asked.

She nodded, withdrawing her hand as quickly as she could. No one called her Stephanie now, aside from her brother. And only then when he was mad with her. Which was, unfortunately, quite often.

'Stephanie is a lovely name,' he said. But the chill in his voice undermined any chance his comment had of being a compliment.

And what, exactly, was he implying about her pseudonym, then? Stephanie ground her teeth even as she maintained her smile and channelled her alter ego.

Steffi Leigh always acted as if anyone could be wrapped around her little finger. Just because this guy looked as if he was made from titanium, it didn't mean she couldn't pretend.

'Shall we snap a selfie to record the moment?' She forced a laugh. In terms of coming up with content, getting pictures for her social media accounts nearly killed her—this would be a good one.

'No.'

Flat. Uncompromising. Unimpressed.

*Way to start, Steffi.* She nibbled the inside of her cheek, momentarily set back. But the 'Steffi Leigh' scene was what he wanted, right? This was the deal—the personality and pop culture vibe was what he wanted to buy.

'No? I'll go solo, then.' She wasn't going to let him crush her. She held out her phone and quickly took a shot. She'd never use it, but he didn't need to know that.

'You do that often?' he asked in a low voice.

'I do whatever it takes.' She smiled at him, refusing to hear the sarcastic, slightly improper thread to his question. 'My followers enjoy my pictures.'

Most of her pictures didn't actually feature *her*—usually she put together some quirky set piece with a new product, or made a meme to amuse.

'Are you going to spend the next two hours tweaking the image with filters and Photoshop?' he asked.

'I don't do that either. Most of my photos are unfiltered.'

He looked at her—another slow appraisal, up and down. 'Yes. That I can believe. You obviously took the two hours to apply filters in real life.'

Actually, that wasn't far from the truth. Her perfectly blended layers of concealer, foundation, blusher, powder and eyeshadow *had* taken Tara almost two hours, and Stephanie was sure it was melting off already.

What was this guy's beef? Why be so pointed when *he* was the one who'd requested this meeting? But she was the one who needed it. So she had to play nice.

'You got me.' Determinedly she kept smiling up at him from between thickly mascaraed lashes.

'What do you look like without it?'

'Even more amazing,' she flipped back at him, unable to stop her irritation sparking.

'I'd like to see that.'

*Never going to happen.*

She glared at him, her eyes locking with his. And, even though she hadn't voiced it, she was certain he knew exactly what she was thinking. He thought she was some painted-up doll and an airhead to boot.

Patronising jerk.

But suddenly, finally, the man smiled.

Stephanie almost gasped in shock as another bolt of electricity kicked through her. If she'd thought him attractive in a ruthless kind of way before, now he was just meltingly gorgeous. He looked younger, more fun, more *mischievous*. Yeah. Total personality transplant.

It might have been better if he'd stayed icy and unimpressed.

'I'm sorry if I've been abrupt,' he said. And he was still totally abrupt, but with that winning smile it didn't seem so rude. 'I was distracted when you first arrived.'

Yeah, and *she* needed distraction now.

*Think, brain. Think.*

Then she remembered she'd made a plan. She'd known there was no way she was going to manage sitting across a table from him for three hours. Steffi Leigh only did twenty-second intros, then used what was around her—products, lists, the totally random—to fill in the time. So she was going to take Jack Wolfe on tour.

'No problem—no one's perfect,' she said smoothly, still inwardly stunned by his apology. 'Look, here comes Tara.' She gestured towards the slim woman walking towards them, mentally muttering thanks to the heavens. 'She's my assistant.'

But Jack didn't look at Tara. He kept his too blue eyes on her.

'We're kidnapping you,' Stephanie added brightly.

'You're kidnapping me.' He glanced down at her dress again. Then looked at himself. Raised one eyebrow. 'You have chloroform with you?'

So there was a size difference. A huge one. But her being small didn't mean she didn't have strength. Or cunning.

'Charm is more effective.' She smiled.

'Charm, you say?' A gleam lit in his eye. 'I'm not sure I'd call what you have *charm*.'

Stephanie's blood heated, but she refused to rise to the bait and ask what it was he *did* think she had. *Not going to do it.* And she was not going to respond to his low, alarmingly sexy chuckle either.

'Tara's our chauffeur for the afternoon,' she told him. Chauffeur, make-up diva, sidekick. Saviour.

'Sorry about that...' Tara breezed towards her, looking down and rubbing her hands. 'There was this hand cream in there that I just *had* to try, only it had—'

'Tara.' Stephanie interrupted quickly. 'This is Jack Wolfe.' The man didn't need to know about Tara's insatiable cosmetics fetish.

'*You're* Jack Wolfe?' Tara finally stopped admiring her hands and looked up at him. Her stunned expression would have been comic if it hadn't been so annoying.that the guy had this effect on everyone?

'I'm afraid so,' he said, with surprising softness. 'Were you expecting someone else?'

'No. You're...perfect as you are.'

'Thank you.' He shot Stephanie a sideways look and echoed even more softly, 'Hear that? *Perfect*.'

Stephanie eyed him coldly and then turned back to Tara.

But Tara's eyes had rounded and she looked from Jack to Stephanie and back again. Her mouth opened. Then closed. And then she smiled.

It wasn't a smile Stephanie trusted.

'Shall I go get the car?' Tara said chirpily. 'I'll bring it to the main entrance.'

Stephanie stared, aghast, as her so-called friend left her alone with the man—*again*.

'Why do we need the car?' Jack asked.

'As I said, we're kidnapping you. You're going on the Steffi Leigh tour of Melbourne.' She pulled on her best smile again. 'You only arrived in Australia this morning, right?' His assistant had sent his schedule to her—all efficiency. And apparently he travelled without an entourage.

He frowned.

'Or would you like to stay in the hotel for high tea instead?' Stephanie's heart sank. 'We can go over the paperwork I've brought…'

'I'm not hungry.'

Really? He looked it. He was about six feet tall, and sharp muscled in a lean way—as if he'd been fed only just enough to maintain optimal performance capability, like a caged cheetah kept on rations, so he'd run world-record-fast for the kill.

'You're sure?' she queried.

He nodded.

'Then that's it.' She smiled between gritted teeth. 'The abduction goes ahead.'

Without waiting for him to say anything more, she turned and walked back across the expansive lobby to the door. Surely she could do the comebacks, put on the charm, maintain the persona just long enough to seal the deal? She was not going to let him annoy her into slipping and lowering her guard again.

'Why can't *you* drive?' he asked, keeping pace alongside her.

'I'm going to be talking to you.' *Selling it to him.*

'I thought women were good at multi-tasking.'

'Actually, I think it's better to focus on one task at a time and do it to the best of your ability.'

'*I'll* drive, then.'

'Excuse me?'

'I'll drive.'

As if Tara was *ever* going to let him near her precious car. And as if he'd want to be seen behind the wheel of it once he saw it.

'Will you be able to *listen* and drive?' Stephanie asked.

'That's going to depend on whether what's being said is interesting enough.'

He'd thrown down the gauntlet now. Stephanie straightened. Could he smell the desperation clinging to her? She couldn't let him see just how badly she wanted this deal.

'*Tara* can drive us,' she said firmly. 'So it's not going to be a problem.'

'Does Tara own the blog or do you?' he asked, and stopped walking. Forcing her to stop and face him.

'I do.'

'Then *you're* the one I need to negotiate with. Only you.'

Insisting on meeting with her alone was unconventional—possibly bordering on unprofessional. But could she really complain when she'd been the one to say she was going to abduct him?

'Can you drive that?' Stephanie gestured at the car turning into the entranceway. The vintage Mercedes convertible in ultra-feminine pale pastel yellow was not a car a man like him would want to drive, surely.

'Where are *you* going to sit?' he asked, looking puzzled.

'In the middle—in the back.'

'You're a contortionist?' He cast a disbelieving gaze at the tiny back seat.

'The size is deceptive,' she muttered, walking out. She wanted to warn Tara about his attempt to change the plan.

But Jack spoke the second Tara cut the engine. 'Steffi's agreed to let *me* drive.'

'She has? Okay.' Tara smiled up from the driver's seat and then unclipped her seat belt and exited the car. 'If you like, I'll stay here and find out what I can about that lotion. It could be a good one to profile, Stef.'

Stephanie wasn't near enough to stab her in the ribs with her index finger. Or stomp discreetly on her toes. But she could glare. 'You don't *mind* not coming?' Stephanie questioned pointedly.

'Not at all.' Tara didn't even look at her as she dropped the car key into Jack's outstretched hand. Instead she smiled at him. 'I'm sure you'll be careful with her.'

Her the car? Or her Steffi?

Jack looked amused. 'I'm always careful.'

Stephanie wanted to kidnap them both and drop them into the Southern Ocean. Instead she acted all Steffi Leigh and stepped in front of Jack to pull Tara into a quick hug.

'Will you check on Dan for me?' she asked quickly into her friend's ear.

She hadn't left her brother alone for as long as this in months.

'Of course.'

As Stephanie stepped back Tara looked too happy for comfort.

'It'll be fine,' Tara added meaningfully.

'You will check, though? In person?'

'Trust me.' Tara leaned forward and wrapped Stephanie in another quick hug. 'What's the worst that can happen?' She stage whispered, 'It's only a couple of hours. Go enjoy yourself.'

How was she supposed to enjoy herself with the wolf?

And yet there was a tightening in her body, as if her muscles had sharpened and her skin had shrunk. As if she was preparing for something.

*Anticipation.*

She hadn't felt it in such a long time. Hadn't looked forward to anything in so long. She was looking forward to negotiating with this man—to taking what she wanted from him. She *was* going to secure this deal, for all his initial disapproval.

'Bye, Jack. Nice to meet you.' Tara waved and practically skipped back into the hotel.

Jack walked around to the driver's door.

'You know we drive on the left side of the road here?' Stephanie muttered grimly.

'I'm aware of that.' He got into the car and slung his briefcase on the back seat.

By the time she got into the passenger seat he already had his seatbelt fastened and was sliding his hands over the steering wheel, getting the feel of the vintage beauty.

'You're *sure* you don't want me to drive?' Stephanie wasn't sure she could cope with sitting so near to him. He seemed bigger, somehow.

His answering smile was not innocent.

Stephanie ignored the traitorous warmth invading her body. She could *not* be attracted to someone so arrogant. 'You don't want to have to listen to me issue directions all the time.'

'We'll get to where we want to be more quickly without directions.'

Without directions? 'You don't know where I'm going to take you.'

'But I know exactly where I want to go.'

She pressed her lips together, understanding. He'd been

to Melbourne before. He had somewhere he wanted to go. So he'd hijacked her abduction plan.

'You don't like ceding control? Always have to be in charge of the destination? Hence your need to write travel guides telling people the best way to get to the best place to go?'

She shouldn't have said that—Steffi Leigh was supposed to be too sweet to get snippy.

'*You're* the one dictating what colour gelato people should eat to look "effortlessly cool",' he mocked. 'As if flavour doesn't matter.'

'You have it wrong. Taste is everything.'

'Is it?' His lips curved. 'What do you suggest *I* taste?'

She was *not* responding to the suggestion in that question. She was ignoring it altogether. 'And there was me thinking that the Wolfe way was to take the route less travelled—to put yourself in the care of the *locals…*' Coolly she spouted his own travel tips at him.

'You want to take care of me?' He laughed.

That genuine sound surprised her into silence. He was a different man from the one she'd first laid eyes on. Had she dreamt the terse way he'd spoken into the phone and that bleak expression? And then that naked hostility? Because now *he* was all charm.

He turned the key and the car purred. Slowly he pulled out into the lane of traffic.

'Who's Dan?' he asked.

She gritted her teeth, holding back the *What business is it of yours?* bite that had leapt to her throat. 'My cat.'

'Cat…?' he echoed. His eyes narrowed on the road ahead. 'You don't look like a cat lady. I'd have thought you'd be a handbag dog diva.'

'*So* last decade,' she murmured. 'And you know I live to subvert your stereotypical assumptions about vapid creatures like me.'

'I never said you were vapid.'

'You didn't have to. It was all in the look.'

'Look?'

'The look you sent me when I first arrived.'

'How did I look at you?'

'Like you couldn't *believe* you were going to have to sit through a boring business meeting with a brainless piece of fluff like me.'

He pulled up at a red light and turned to meet her eyes. 'How am I looking at you now?'

Meeting his eyes, she couldn't think at all. Then she remembered his contortionist comment and his taste comment and saw the unrestrained provocation in his eyes. 'Like you're hungrier than you claim to be.'

An electrical charge pulsed in the resulting silence.

'All big eyes and sharp teeth?' he finally responded. 'You're afraid I'm the Big Bad Wolf?'

'Aren't you?'

'You're confusing me with my brother George. I'm no wolf—not really.' For a second that bleakness flashed into his eyes again, but he blinked and it was gone.

'How disappointing,' Stephanie murmured.

'You were looking forward to the chase?' he challenged. 'Did you *want* to be caught and devoured?'

'I was looking forward to running away.' As she answered she realised it wasn't a mere Steffi Leigh comeback but the honest truth. She *had* been looking forward to running away for a couple hours this afternoon. Escaping her tiny flat, her brother, her blog. Taking Jack Wolfe on a tour had been an excuse, so she wouldn't feel guilty about walking out for a little while.

He looked at her more thoughtfully. More intensely. 'You surprise me.'

'I'm so pleased,' she replied, far too politely. And far too falsely even for Steffi Leigh.

'Stephanie—' He broke off at the sound of a phone ringing.

He looked at the phone, his face becoming that rigid mask again as he glanced at the name on the screen. 'Excuse me a moment. I need to take this.'

He pulled over to the side of the road, ignoring the blare of the horn from the car behind.

'Well?' he asked tersely. There was a moment as the caller replied. Then, 'Fine. I'll be there.'

Jack tucked his phone inside his jacket pocket, but didn't pull back into the line of traffic. His hand on the steering wheel clenched into a fist. Stephanie ran her tongue over her dried lips, unsure whether or not to speak. She knew he was looking at her—she wasn't sure she wanted to look back at him.

Finally she did, and was instantly caught in the swirling blue storm of his eyes. That rawness was back—intense banked emotion, threatening to surge and spill. That electrical current spiked between them again.

'Steffi Leigh…' he murmured slowly, using her blogging name. 'Do you *really* want to run away?'

# CHAPTER TWO

THE QUESTION WASN'T all innocent, but Jack Wolfe couldn't bring himself to regret it.

Or to apologise.

Not as he watched the emotions flicker in her big eyes. For a second she looked startled, but then fire flashed in those blue-green, draw-you-in depths. A sizzle sparked under his collar in response. He realised he was holding his breath—*seriously*? As if her answer mattered *that* much?

He blinked, trying to pull his wayward brain back to reality, but for a moment it seemed she actually was contemplating an escape with him. As if the two of them could run away together and steal time alone in the heat?

His body grew hotter. His skin tighter.

But then, as he watched, that polite veneer of hers descended. Back to frosted—*frosty*—perfection. Disappointment trickled, cooling his jets. He'd bet she was like one of those ornate overpriced cupcakes people queued for at fashionable boutiques. A tempting confection, smothered in layers of intricate icing, beautifully presented...but when it came to the tasting there was very little cake.

Jack liked cake. Icing...? Not so much.

'Do you?' Her voice was low, but there was the slightest of catches in it. An edge.

Was this how she was determined to play it? To be 'nice' and 'accommodating' and turn everything back to *his* wishes? Was she that eager to impress—to please? To secure this deal?

Would she say yes to anything he offered or asked?

For a moment he was tempted, so tempted, to ask for everything he shouldn't.

Because, *yes*. He wanted to run away. And right now he wanted to run away with *her*.

Instead, he drew a steadying breath and answered. 'Always.'

The spark in her eyes reignited. *Defiance*.

'Because your life is so dreadful?' she asked.

'Everyone has their challenges,' he answered coolly.

Another emotion, frostier than ever, entered her eyes. She thought he was spoilt. Inwardly he laughed at the irony. This was a woman who spent her life online, talking about new perfumes and places to party.

'Yes, it must be tough producing all those travel pieces. Getting to go to the furthest corners of the planet...' she murmured.

Nowadays too much of his time was spent chained to a desk in one of many offices Wolfe Enterprises had around the world. It was his underlings and contractors who got to see the actual sights.

But he wasn't about to try to prove himself to her. She could think what she liked. In fact, he was pleased she wasn't the total yes-girl he'd had her pegged as.

So he smiled at the sceptical expression she was failing to hide from him. 'Don't you have things *you* want to escape from at times?' he asked, keeping his focus on her unbelievably beautiful face.

If her make-up weren't so bulletproof he'd guess there would be colour running into her cheeks. She licked her lips in a nervous gesture that—inexcusably—turned him on.

Now was *not* the time for his body to go renegade. Steffi Leigh was everything Jack Wolfe didn't want in a woman. She was a high-maintenance, shallow 'stylista', dictating to the rest of the world what to eat, what to wear, where to go and what to talk about. All instruction given in that relentlessly positive, upbeat, *girly* way. Did she even believe half the stuff she spouted? She was the kind of candy usually hanging off his brother George's arm.

Though he had to concede she wasn't as vapid as she looked. She wasn't afraid to needle him a little. Yeah... surprisingly Steffi Leigh was not *entirely* nice. And that appealed more than it should. Now he wanted to peel back those perfect layers and find the essence of her. He suspected it wasn't purely vanilla.

'Stephanie?' he prompted a little roughly, feeling the urge to spar harder with her. How far would he have to push to make her ditch that relentlessly smiling persona and snap at him?

*He* was *not* nice today.

'No.' She smiled. 'Not at all.'

That overly determined answer both annoyed and amused him. He knew to his bones she wasn't being honest. He'd irritated her, but she wasn't going to bite back. Which made her better than him. Because he was close to snapping.

'*No?*' he asked, letting his disbelief show.

She continued to meet his gaze with a defiant little tilt to her chin. He fell silent, falling into the spell she seemed to cast wordlessly—all with those big blue-green eyes that made his skin burn.

For too long he looked at her. Desire sank deeper into his muscles, slicing through to the bone. What he'd do to make her mask slip—

But then his damn phone beeped, signalling a new text message. He didn't read it, but the sound alone was enough to make reality race back.

He cleared his throat. 'Where were you planning to take me?' Time to pull back and be professional—focus on the far more important meeting he had in two days' time. 'Some new mall? A new consumer paradise?'

'Not a mall, no.'

*Thank God.* But he faked a crestfallen look. 'That's a shame. I wanted to see you in action.'

'I'm sorry?' Her eyes widened.

He bit back a grin. It was obvious she'd heard inappropriate innuendo when he hadn't meant it. *Interesting.*

'I wanted to see how you come up with all your content,' he clarified with an easy smile. 'How you create all those lists and pictures…'

'Oh…' She nodded. 'Well, there are a couple of out-of-the-way places I thought it would be nice for you to see. They're upcoming features on the blog.' She bestowed her wide 'Steffi Leigh' smile upon him. 'So your wish will be granted.'

As if she was some fairy princess? *Yeah.* That was *totally* how she sold herself. A bright, bubbly bringer of beauty and joy.

'What about your office?' he asked. 'Where you film your vlogs? I'd like to see that.'

He wanted to see what was on the other side of the camera—what it was that wasn't shown on screen. Because his curiosity had been aroused—along with a few other things.

'You want to see my room?' She shifted, lifting a hand to adjust her seatbelt as if it were strapping her in too tightly.

For a split second she looked startled. In fact, he'd go so far as to say she looked scared. But then she released the belt and put that smile back on her face.

'I'm sorry—not today.'

She wasn't sorry, and now he really *did* want to see her space. What was all this icing hiding?

'Actually, I was going to take you to the zoo,' she suddenly spoke again, looking down at her lap.

'The zoo?'

'Perfect place for you,' she murmured.

'Pardon?'

'Have you ever seen a baby echidna?' She lifted her lashes, her eyes now limpid. 'They're very cute.'

'Cute?' He couldn't decide if her eyes were more green than blue or more blue than green. All he really knew was that the colour was natural. He was close enough to know she wasn't wearing contacts. 'I don't do cute.'

Whereas *she* did nothing but.

'Do you even know what an echidna is?' she asked.

'A small, strange-looking thing that's one of the very few mammals that lays eggs,' he replied. He did travel guidebooks for a living—he knew random facts about animals in so many countries. 'Is that why you're wearing gloves? So you don't get your hands dirty while you feed the cute little animals?'

For a moment she didn't answer. But her gaze sharpened, held his ensnared. Was it him, or was it getting hotter? The temperature was *searing*.

Finally, pointedly, she lifted her eyebrows. 'You think I'm afraid of getting dirty?'

Her reply sounded *so* innocuous. But that glimmer in her eyes... She'd turned some innuendo on *him*. Turned him on tighter...

He glanced up at the crystalline sky above, taking a breather from the intensity. They'd got barely two blocks from the hotel and he couldn't be more on edge. Who'd have thought she'd pack such a punch?

'Why else the gloves?' He couldn't resist glancing back at her.

She eyed him thoughtfully. 'I'm wearing gloves to hide the state of my fingernails.'

'You're not happy with the colour of the polish? Does it clash with the car?' he mocked.

'Don't tell anyone...' She leaned a touch closer to him

and spoke with a conspiratorial smile. 'But they're bitten down to the quick and I didn't get the chance to put on fake ones.'

Honesty? It almost touched him—except she was all about covering up.

'You're wearing other fake things?' He couldn't help a glance to her chest. *His bad*. He owned it, but he figured she'd started it.

She pulled back to settle into the farthest corner of her seat. 'A woman never gives up *all* her secrets.'

'No? Only enough to engender interest?' he taunted. 'Is that one of the tips you dish out on your blog?'

She smiled a secretive, frankly seductive fairy princess smile. 'My tips are *very* popular.'

That they were. And he could see why. She could write—her lists were entertaining. But it was the vlogs that had the greatest number of hits. It seemed people liked watching her prance about in her bedroom. His body winched tighter.

'You're interested in wildlife?' And, yeah, he might have emphasised the 'wild' just a little.

'Most people are.' She continued to smile at him—so innocent and perky. Except for that heat in the back of her eyes. 'And I thought you'd like to see some that's unique to Australia. We have some amazing creatures. There's a very big saltwater crocodile at the zoo. I think you'd like him. I'm sure he'd like *you*.'

He chuckled, appreciating the less than subtle implication. 'I'm tougher than I look. Can't be chewed up and spat out as easily as all that.'

'Oh?' She sounded disbelieving. 'So you don't want to go to the zoo? Where *do* you want to run away to?'

*Anywhere. As long as it was with her.*

He looked at her silently, trying to ride out the intense impulse sweeping over him. The car seemed to be shrinking. She was so near he saw her breath hitch, heard that faintest gasp. The urge to kiss her was overwhelming.

*Sex.* The body's happy place. And for him the ultimate avoidance activity. He'd bury himself in her hot, tight body and screw their brains out. Until he could think of nothing else. Until he was exhausted and could sleep—not lie awake for hours and hours and hours, wondering and worrying and worrying and worrying…

It wasn't such a bad idea, was it?

Wrong. It was the worst idea ever. He hadn't succeeded as much as he had by bedding possible business partners.

He'd *never* done that.

Steffi Leigh was the excuse he'd given for making this trip to Australia. His brothers had been on his back about working too hard, but he'd said he needed to assess the viability of this acquisition himself. Truth was, he was hunting for something far more personal and he didn't want to hurt his family by telling them yet. Not until he knew for sure. Not until he'd found everything out—even if it was the worst.

'Jack…?' A soft query.

He'd been silent too long—staring…all but eating her with his eyes. And in her eyes now was not just that spark that lit brighter as he neared, but the concern he'd turned away from the first moment he'd seen her.

She'd seen his anxiety again. And he hated it just as much as he had in the hotel foyer.

Unable to take the heat any more, Jack shrugged off his jacket and tossed it onto the ludicrously small back seat of the femininely sweet car.

Her eyes widened. 'What are you doing?'

'I'm hot.' *No lie.* And it wasn't because of the sun beating down on them.

He loosened his tie. Then thought better of it and took it off entirely, lying it on top of his jacket. Then he undid the top two buttons of his shirt, undid the cufflinks and rolled his sleeves to just below his elbows.

'Do you mind?' he asked as he worked.

'Of course not.'

But not even the make-up could mask her blush now.

So he wasn't the only one feeling it.

He knew that. Knew there was no way she wasn't feeling the electricity arcing between them.

His phone beeped again. Sighing, he twisted to retrieve it from his jacket pocket and glanced at the screen to read the message. His private investigator had gone all efficient and diarised their meeting for him.

Reading it in black and white, he felt his lungs tighten. As did every one of his muscles. Anxiety returned in an unexpected tsunami. He gritted his teeth. He'd travelled the world over—going into war zones, danger zones, crossing arid deserts and ice floes. But he'd never felt as freaked out as he had when he'd taken that call ten minutes ago. As he did now.

But he'd been waiting over twenty years for this meeting—what was another forty-eight hours?

*Torture.* That was what it was. Pure, poisonous torture.

And hell, yes, he wanted to run away for the duration.

He needed time to speed up. Needed something else to think about for the next day or two or he was going to go insane.

Unable to help himself, he looked at her again and drank in the sight of her strawberry blonde hair, so intricately curled and coiled against her head, and her flawless pale complexion. Her eyes were bright, her lips glossy, and her petite figure was shown off to perfection in that pressed mint-green dress.

She didn't look exactly like the profile picture on her blog. She looked better. It was the spark in her eyes. Not the make-up and the 'look-but-don't-touch' dress, but the

underlying attitude. That hint of something more dangerous within her—the certainty that she was keeping part
of herself back.

He found her as irritating and as attractive as hell.

Yeah, he'd do anything to avoid thinking about that
meeting. Absolutely anything. And *everything*.

He'd bite through those layers of rich, sweet icing. There
was definitely more substance—more cake—than he'd first
thought. And he *did* like cake.

But it wasn't all about him. He wanted to see her fall into
it—fall apart. He wanted to watch her eyes glaze and her
cheeks redden without the aid or the mask of make-up. He
wanted to see her sweaty and wet and flushed and laughing. And then crying her release. He wanted her mindless
and begging to be tipped over the edge. He wanted to be
the one to make her.

*So* inappropriate. Borderline insane. Sexual harassment
stuff.

He *had* to rein it in.

It wasn't as if he hadn't had sex in years. He enjoyed
holiday affairs with women who didn't know who he was.
When they found out he moved on. They were a short escape from his real world.

He wanted to escape *now*. He wanted to scoop her up
and toss her into the nearest swimming pool so he could
see her clearly. He wanted to see her *wet*.

The urge to provoke her was irresistible. The urge to
touch her he was restraining. *Just.*

Because he hadn't lied. Jack Wolfe *wasn't* like his play-
boy brother George. Or his bona fide hero James.

Truth was, they weren't related at all. And *there* was the
cause of the ache. He was no Wolfe.

'Are you going to answer that?' she asked, her soft voice
rasping.

His phone was ringing.

She watched him. No expression creased that immaculately painted face. But in her eyes all was emotion—all concern.

He hated it. He wanted nothing but that heat again.

He forced himself to tear his attention away from her. Glancing down, he read his brother's name on the screen.

'No,' he said shortly.

He wasn't going to answer. He couldn't speak to his brother at this moment without giving himself away. If his brother heard his anxiety he'd be hounding him for the reason. And Jack wasn't ready to explain it yet. But the second his phone stopped ringing it chimed to signal another text message.

'Busy guy.'

He put his phone on the back seat again. 'I run a company. "Busy" comes with the territory.'

A phone chimed. Hers this time.

'Do you mind?' She echoed his words as she opened her small bag.

'Not at all.' He watched as she quickly scanned the screen, a very faint frown pulling at her eyebrows. 'Busy blogger?'

'Of course. As you know, my audience is global. People like to have their comments acknowledged.'

'So you're always on call?'

'Not for just anyone.' She sent him a look. 'Only my followers.'

He smiled, finding her slight snarkiness oddly soothing. 'Your fans?'

'People who like what I do,' she said proudly. 'I like to keep them happy.'

'You're not out to please everyone, then?'

'We all know that's impossible. We all know the internet has plenty of haters lurking behind anonymity.'

He didn't like the idea of haters hating her. Even though he'd come close to it himself.

'I perform for my crowd,' she said.

'And that's what it is? Purely a performance?'

Caution clouded her eyes. 'I believe in what I do.'

So did a lot of people, given how popular she was. Her blog and video channel transcended borders. Her audience went way beyond Melbourne—beyond Australia, even. Apparently *millions* of young women hung on her every word. And she had plenty of words. There were lists on what not to wear, on make-up, movies. On where to eat, what to eat… There were commentaries on celebrity outfits during the awards season. She had people clicking on her blog as she provided chat through movie awards, music awards…

It was a bright, bubbly mash-up of lifestyle, design and travel tips, geared towards the urban young woman. The segment of the market *his* company wanted greater engagement with.

Jack had read only a couple of her blogs and watched mere seconds of one video before switching it off in annoyance at the over-the-top girlish effervescence. But he'd relied on the advice of his researchers that Steffi Leigh was *it*. Apparently making enough money not to need a real job. And yet she wanted this deal.

That was why she was determined to be nice to him. Even when she didn't really want to be. Which told him that she needed this sale to go ahead. *Badly.*

Why *was* that? Did she need the money to fund her lifestyle? Her purchases? He'd wanted to know why—within five minutes of meeting her he now wanted to know everything.

What he *didn't* want was an afternoon of traipsing around while she fed him bubbly tips, trying to close the sale. He wanted to cut to the chase and understand the reality.

'What if I took *you* somewhere?' he asked.

'As you've insisted on driving, I'd assumed that was happening already. By the way, I'm *loving* being parked illegally for so long.'

Suddenly Jack knew exactly what he was going to do. A long drive in a vintage convertible with a beautiful woman beside him was every man's fantasy, right?

It wouldn't be the first time for Jack, but he had the feeling it was going to be the most fun.

'We're going to be little longer than we scheduled,' he said unapologetically. 'But it'll be worth it.'

Her polite façade tilted. 'I'm sorry, I can't stay longer than we initially scheduled.'

'Why not? Is there some place you've got to be? Some new restaurant opening?' He wondered if she'd answer honestly.

Her smile remained fixed. 'No, but—'

'There's no problem, then.' He didn't give her time to argue. 'We can escape.'

'I've already told you I don't need to escape anything in my life.'

'*Everyone* needs to escape some time.'

She looked at him, her eyes narrowing. But she didn't answer. Didn't lie. She *did* want to run away—and not really from him. There were things in her life she wanted to escape.

'You want me to buy your blog?' he asked.

Her lips parted. 'Are you blackmailing me?'

He wasn't, actually, but it was interesting that she'd leapt to that conclusion. She definitely had thoughts on the darker side.

'All I meant was that we might talk at length about the deal on our drive. I find driving helps me think. And make decisions.'

She still hesitated.

He was used to people saying yes. Spoilt, perhaps, but there it was. He was used to asking and receiving. In terms of business and in terms of women. But it was only because of what they could get from him in return. And that wasn't emotion. It was cash. Or connections. Or both.

'There's a retreat I have to take a look at.' He was booked to stay there after his day in the city. He'd bring his stay forward a night.

'A retreat?' she queried.

He nodded. 'It would be a good source of inspiration for your blog. You can take a look around and show me how you'd put it all together online.'

Truth was the Green Veranda wasn't right for her blog. Nor was it going into one of the Wolfe travel guides. It was too expensive, and already too exclusive to need it. It catered to a celebrity clientele, or the über-wealthy who didn't want attention from the general public or any intrusion. Solitude and privacy guaranteed.

Jack didn't want that level of isolation and introspection now—not with these two days stretching before him like purgatory. No, he needed distraction.

And he had it sitting right beside him.

'A retreat as in…like a health spa?' she asked.

'Sort of. A very expensive private hotel. You can stay the night, yes?' The idea was growing on him with every second.

'Stay the *night*?' she echoed.

He laughed at the hint of horror in her voice. He'd let her off that hook a little later—for now it was too much fun taking in her reaction. Wickedly amused, he watched her internal war—whether to breathe yes or snap no?

Her blush deepened as she gazed back at him, her eyes as huge and as brilliant as the sky above them. Spark, heat, defiance, indecision. He swore he could almost hear her pulse racing. His own heart quickened in response.

In the end he decided to take the burden from her.

'Sure.' He smiled as he put the car in gear and pulled back into the line of traffic. 'Because *I'm* kidnapping *you*.'

# CHAPTER THREE

JACK WOLFE DIDN'T need either chloroform or charm to get what he wanted—he had *cash*.

Because of the possibilities he represented, Stephanie couldn't refuse him. And now she knew he wasn't afraid to take advantage of the fact. She also knew he had a wicked streak—an impulsiveness she'd never have expected from the grim-looking man she'd first laid eyes on.

*Stay the night?* Never.

The car sped along the road, taking the quickest route out of the city. The sun beat down on her, addling her brain. Or maybe the sizzling heat was emanating from *him*. With his tie removed and his shirtsleeves rolled, some of his body was exposed. The muscles in his forearms flexed and she could see the strength in his large hands as he handled the delicate, sometimes temperamental vintage car assuredly.

He made it look easy, when she knew for a fact that it wasn't.

But to indulge in the utter fantasy of being in this dress, in this car, next to him, for an hour or so of illicit escape…

'No choice,' she muttered.

A small, wicked smile played on his lips. It seemed he'd taken the brakes off both the car *and* himself, leaving him relaxed and carefree and so strikingly attractive it was a wonder she could breathe.

'Stephanie…' he drawled softly. 'There should *always* be a choice.' He glanced her way, a half-question in the back of his blue eyes.

Stephanie licked her dried lips. She could say no. Could

demand that he turn around and take her back to the hotel immediately. If she insisted he'd acquiesce. He wasn't about to abduct her for real. Not for a whole night.

But what a choice it was—stay and play along with his whim, or go and kiss goodbye to any chance of the deal happening?

As she looked at him time stopped. There was that unspoken communication—that intensity that she wanted to run from yet couldn't break. *Fascination.* She wanted to be near him for longer. Was this what it was like for her mother when she went headlong into her latest affair?

Stephanie shivered, almost repulsed by her intense reaction to him.

When her oxygen-deprived brain decided to reinstate the use of her vocal cords she answered his question with one of her own. 'Do you know where you're going?'

'I have a rough idea.' His wicked smile went on full wattage. He looked outrageously pleased with himself. And devastatingly attractive.

She'd bet he knew *exactly* where he was going. Even in that moment of distress she'd seen back at the hotel he'd been decisive, confident. And determined.

The car sped faster down the motorway and Stephanie slipped into the realisation of a long-held private fantasy—*not* knowing where she was going. For years she'd dreamed of randomly picking a road and driving along it for as far as she felt like. Or letting someone *else* take her for a ride for as far and as long as she wanted…

Sweet temptation accelerated along her veins. She'd always wanted to 'up and leave'—see where the wind blew her. Had always yearned to go deep into the dry heart of the country and explore the infinite unknown possibilities…

Except the one time she'd tried she'd almost destroyed what little was left of her family.

*Dan.*

Cold memories slammed into her. Her mistakes burned, and regret tasted as acid and as fresh as the day disaster had struck.

She felt responsible for her brother's disabilities. Every single one of the golden possibilities he'd had had been destroyed. Dan had gone from sporting superstar to wheelchair-bound and broken. His future had once been assured. Now it was up to her to assure him a different future.

He was the reason she was here now.

So she shouldn't be ogling Jack's powerful-looking hands or feeling tantalised by his smile. She wasn't here to flirt. She needed to focus. And she needed to check on her brother ASAP.

Her fingers tightened on her mobile phone. She'd send a quick, quiet text to Dan and another to Tara to double-check her brother was okay.

Jack *wasn't* finding out about her brother. She wasn't telling him *he* was the reason why she couldn't be out for hours and hours. She was *not* playing the pity card. She'd keep up her 'take it or leave it' aura—the projection that she had no worries, no *need* of his offer, was key. She didn't want him thinking she *had* to sell her site. She couldn't appear desperate.

But in truth she'd do whatever it took to secure Dan's future.

As she texted, Jack's phone rang again. He didn't bother to pull over and answer it this time. If anything, it felt as if he hit the accelerator more heavily.

'Tell me more about your blog. You write all kinds of lists, right?' he said, talking loudly over the top of his incessant ringtone.

'That's how it started, yes,' she answered, still looking down at her own phone.

Her blog was still titled 'The List'. She'd begun with all kinds of crazy lists, but the lists had really been a cover for random comments on everyday absurdities to entertain her friends. It had evolved from there, although now they were more straight lists than any kind of astute commentaries, but she tried to keep them as fun and entertaining as always.

'Because lists are catchy?' he asked. '"Ten Ways with a Tank Top" or something?'

'Or something…' she murmured. 'Lists are easy and quick to read, and people like them. They're popular. It's that simple.'

'Do you write lists for *everything*?'

The tips of her ears burned as she thought she caught an intimate nuance in his voice. Was he thinking *personal* lists?

She sent him a sharp look and registered his amusement.

She turned back to glare at the bitumen ahead. She *wasn't* biting. But, sure, she could list a number of things she'd like to do with him—none of them polite. Not all of them strictly businesslike and professional either.

'Yes!' She made herself reply in ultra-perky Steffi Leigh style. 'They help me stay organised.'

'So, do you have a list of everything you're going to achieve in life?'

'Like many of your travellers will have a list of all the must-do, must-see places—of course.'

'I'm curious about what's on it.'

'Oh, you know—the usual stuff anyone has.'

'I can't believe that. I get the impression you're not like just "anyone".'

'I'll take that as a compliment.' She laughed. *Pure* Steffi Leigh.

'Tell me about the haters. How do you handle them?'

'I don't,' she said, her amusement fading. 'I ignore them.'

'It's that easy?'

It was *never* that easy. 'To be honest, I let a lot of my

hard-core fans respond to them. I used to moderate the comments, but it took up too much time.'

'But you still read them all?'

'Yes.'

'And it doesn't get to you?'

'Why would I let it?' She maintained her smile with determination. 'There are far more positive comments than negative. *They're* the ones I think about when I'm working on a segment.'

At first the blog had been for her own fun. Then it had grown legs of its own—until she'd been sprinting to try to keep up with its demands. Since Dan's illness it had got harder to maintain the schedule, and yet she had all the more reason to make it bigger and better. Leveraging her 'platform' was the only way she could think of to earn the money she needed to get her brother motivated and into some kind of study.

She waited, but Jack still ignored the strident ringing of his phone.

'So your lists cover everything—no topic is off-limits? How do you decide the content? By strategy or whim?' He glanced at her. 'Don't get me wrong—I'm not criticising. I'm trying to understand your success.'

Because it was so hard for him to believe little ol' her could have made something so massive?

How could she be *so* attracted to someone *so* irritating? She had *not* got out enough in the last eighteen months.

'Well…' She smiled another Steffi Leigh smile through gritted teeth, determined to stay positive and upbeat. 'There's a lot of hair and make-up stuff going on. And fashion choices—what to wear, how to wear it. And, yes, there's some whimsy—designing doilies from paper towels or sewing slippers from comic book covers…whatever takes my mind. But I do plan and keep a list of topics—'

'Of course you do.'

'Right.' She conceded another laugh. 'And of course there's restaurant recommendations,' she concluded. 'And good places to go.'

'You make it sound easy, when we both know it isn't,' he commented.

And, stupidly, that was enough to make her feel all warm about him again.

'What's the best trip you've been on?' he asked.

She hesitated, thinking of that fateful holiday to the Northern Territory. For once Dan hadn't had a sporting camp or competition and they'd been able to go. It had been perfect—until his fever and headache had suddenly come on. She'd loved the vast, isolated beauty. But she couldn't bear the reminder of it now.

'I love the big city thrill of Sydney.' She reverted to an answer he'd expect from Steffi Leigh.

'And the shopping?'

'Why, yes…' she all but cooed. 'And all those restaurants. The scene is a lot of fun.'

'And beyond Australia?'

She shrugged. 'I've not been many places outside of Australia.'

She'd not been *anywhere* outside Australia, despite her mum now living in France with husband number three. Because, unlike her mum, she wouldn't walk out on her whole world for a man. Unlike her mum she wouldn't walk out on her responsibilities. And Dan needed someone. By default it had to be her.

That fateful trip Outback had been the first Stephanie had planned—her choice, her organisation—and she'd been so excited because, yes, she'd longed to travel. But Dan had been recovering from the flu just before they'd left and his immunity had been weak. And when they'd been miles from anywhere he'd suddenly got really, really sick.

Headache. Fever. *Rash.*

Stephanie had never been so afraid. Her brother had almost lost his life. As it was the meningitis had cost him limbs—his lower arm, his leg. All his dreams of sporting fame and fortune had been obliterated.

And all because *she'd* been the one who'd insisted on their trip to the back of beyond—where medical help was hours away.

'But what about Queenstown, New Zealand? You had a list on that just the other day on your blog.'

Jack interrupted her thoughts.

Frowning, she glanced at him—and registered his frown. *Queenstown?*

Oh, yes. Her face burned as she suddenly remembered. A schoolfriend had emailed and helped her. She was *so* close to being caught out right now.

'Oh, you know—I meant further afield than New Zealand,' she recovered quickly. 'I meant Europe.'

'Mmm...' he nodded, negotiating an exit onto a different motorway. 'The travel pieces on your blog are done well. You can tell you've spent some time in the places.'

Well, *someone* had. That person just wasn't always *her*.

Tara helped her with the make-up lists, and a few of her other school and uni friends helped her with the destination and restaurant lists. Other stuff she gleaned from the internet.

The truth was that Steffi Leigh was a phony—a caricature of a woman, and not even the author of all the ideas she shared.

So she had to be more careful in answering him. If he knew she faked it—that she got as much help as she did to generate content—he wouldn't be interested in buying the blog at all.

'I haven't covered many destinations outside of Australia,' she said brightly. 'I guess that's something your people could build on if you decide to take it over.'

'Possibly.'

She fidgeted with her phone, absently rubbing her gloved thumb back and forth over the screen, wishing Tara or Dan would hurry up and text back to let her know all was okay.

'What about you?' She flipped the question back at him to fill the lull. 'What was your most amazing adventure? You must have had so many.' And, yes, she *was* envious.

'It's a thing in our family to take a year out to travel. Nothing but a backpack and a few hundred dollars. 'Bye-bye—see you in a year'.'

'Really? No big money? No five-star hotels?' she teased.

'None.'

*Wow.* Curiosity piqued, she twisted to look at him. 'Where did you go?'

'I didn't travel around as much as my brothers did when they went. I spent most of my time in South East Asia. A little village in Indonesia.'

'Working?'

'Volunteering,' he corrected. 'At an orphanage.'

'Doing "the charity thing"?' A tiny thread of jealousy tinted her tone.

'Is that cynicism I hear from Steffi Leigh? Is it so awful to want to help others?'

Of course not. And cynicism wasn't what she'd intended. But now he'd heard it the only thing she could do was make a joke of it. 'So you did your year and now your conscience is salved? You can spend the rest of your life doing the five-star thing?'

'Answer me this, Ms Five Ways with Ugly Festive Woollens, do *you* do charity work?'

'Sure.' *Charity begins at home.* But she played up the flippant. 'A cocktail party. A fundraising dinner. Art auctions. You know how it goes…'

And she was *so* faking it now. She'd never been part of that wealthy socialite do-gooder scene.

'Perhaps.' He glanced at her, his eyes glinting brighter than the sun.

*Possibly. Perhaps.* Full of the non-committal, wasn't he?

'That's your phone again.' She grimaced as it rang loudly yet again.

'You can't cope with the fact I won't answer it?'

'Isn't it rude?'

'Isn't it more rude to sit texting while we're trying to have a conversation?' He nodded pointedly at the phone in her hand. '*You're* the one addicted to your phone. Updating your social media status every two seconds?'

'I was letting Tara know I'm going to be a little late, otherwise she'd worry. Don't *you* check in with family when you travel?'

'No.'

'Well, someone wants you *now*.'

That grim look hardened the line of his mouth. Whoever it was, he was fully into avoidance. And what was the betting it was a woman?

Irritation spurted. 'What if it's an emergency?' she prompted.

'It's not.'

'How can you tell?'

'Because we have a special ringtone for emergencies.'

For a half-second she gaped at him. 'You're making that up.'

'Yes, I am.'

'What if someone is worried about you?'

That oddly tense look crossed his face just has his phone started ringing again. 'I can't answer it. In case you haven't noticed, I'm *driving*.'

'You want me to answer it?' she asked, not meaning it at all.

Suddenly he smiled. 'Would you mind? That'd be great.'

*Huh?* He'd called her bluff.

'Fine.' She twisted to get his phone from where it lay on the tiny back seat, swiping the screen to answer it. 'Jack Wolfe's phone—this is Steffi Leigh speaking. How may I help you?' she asked in dulcet tones.

'Uh…pardon me?'

*Yep. A woman.* Stephanie's blood simmered. 'This is Jack Wolfe's phone… Steffi Leigh speaking,' she repeated. *Ultra*-dulcet.

'Uh, hi… Steffi. Is Jack there? Can I speak to him?'

Definitely a woman. A young, breathless woman, desperate to speak to him.

'I'm sorry,' Stephanie said slowly, 'he's driving at the moment, and the vehicle we're in doesn't have any kind of hands-free capability. Can I take a message for you?'

'Uh, yes, please… This is Bella.'

*Bella.* Nice name for a lover. What was the betting she was tall and slender and stunning—?

'Can you tell him that the board is waiting for that report and they're really pressuring me for a date.' Bella sounded apologetic. 'I know he doesn't want to be disturbed, because he's really busy over there, but they want to know his thoughts as soon as possible. They won't make a decision without his input.'

Huh? *Not* a personal call.

'Also, he's had a zillion messages,' Bella added. 'I've tried to prioritise, and I've put most of them off 'til he's back next week, but the Italian printing company are really pushing to speak with him. Tell him I'm almost out of options for holding them off. The others I've listed in an email to his private account. If he can go through that when he has a minute that would be great.'

'Okay—anything more?' Steffi asked, wanting to get off the phone now.

'Actually, yes…' Bella sounded ultra-apologetic. 'That freelance photographer has been phoning every morning since last Thursday, desperate for an answer on the shots he sent over. I know Jack wants to review them personally, so if he can take a quick look that would be fantastic, because I know he doesn't want to lose him to any competitor if he turns out to be any good. Oh, and the couple who are doing the revision to the French cycling route had all their gear stolen when they were waiting for a train. They're covered with insurance, of course, but now the local mayor is on us because he's worried his town is going to get a bad report. He won't settle for speaking to anyone but Jack. And—'

'Okay, I've got that—thanks, Bella. I've got to go now—sorry. We're about to go into a tunnel and I'll lose reception. Thanks. Bye!'

She touched the screen, ending the call. Then counted to twenty before she dared glance at Jack.

'Tunnel?' Jack asked idly, his attention apparently fully focused on the clear, tunnel-free road ahead.

'Um, that was Bella. I'm guessing she's your PA?' Stephanie took a deep breath. 'She said that the board is—'

'Don't worry—I heard most of it,' he interrupted. 'I'll deal with it later.'

She almost felt like apologising to him herself. 'Sounds like you have a lot going on.'

'Always do. But so do you.' He glanced pointedly at the phone in her other hand—the one that was now buzzing.

Stephanie tensed, then immediately relaxed when she read the text from Tara.

All good this end. Don't worry. Have fun. Do everything I'd do and more.

She chuckled inwardly. There was *nothing* Tara wouldn't do if *she* was sitting next to a man as hot as Jack Wolfe.

She started to tap out a text back.

'Can't you live without your phone for even a few hours?' he asked, sounding touchy.

'Sure I can,' she declared recklessly, happy now she knew all was okay.

'Then I'll tell you what,' he said, suddenly all brusque authority. 'Open up that glove compartment and put your phone there. Put mine in too. And put them both on mute before you do it.'

That was an order if ever she heard one. The CEO in him was making an appearance. 'Seriously?'

'Deadly.'

She didn't need to look at him to know he meant it. She kind of didn't blame him for wanting to escape, given the litany of requests Bella had heaped on him. But she couldn't put her phone in there. She needed to stay in touch with Tara and Dan in case he needed her. But she didn't want to tell Jack that. And, given she'd just heard that all was okay from Tara—

'You're not allowed to touch your phone and nor am I,' said Jack. 'Not for the next six hours. Not if they ring or beep or spontaneously combust.'

'*Six* hours?' They were going to be out *that* long?

'Two hours to get there, two hours to look around, two hours to get back,' he said shortly. 'That okay?'

'I… I guess.' It was better than staying the night, right?

'And all with no phone. First to cave loses.'

'Loses what?'

His sudden unexpected smile was too wicked for her liking.

'What you *should* be asking is what the winner receives.'

She turned in her seat, her heart drumming heavy metal style. 'What do you win if I cave?'

'A taste.'

'Of…?'

'What do you think?' he asked, too softly.

'My blog is ready to be bought, but *I'm* not on the table, Mr Wolfe,' she breathed, trying to be icy. And failing.

'Not yet—and it's Jack.'

'Not *ever*, Mr Wolfe.'

'You're afraid I'll bite? I won't. I'm talking one kiss.'

She stared at him. He was driving along as if he hadn't a care in the world. As if he hadn't just suggested something so wildly inappropriate. Or so wildly tempting.

Finally he glanced over at her. 'You can't tell me you haven't considered the idea already?'

'Your looks have gone to your head.' And thank heavens she had inches of make-up on to hide her flaming cheeks.

'You think I'm good-looking?'

'Your *power* has gone to your head,' she corrected, ignoring him. 'And you're being inappropriate.'

'*My* power?' He looked oh-so-baffled. 'But you're the one who has the thing I want, right? So doesn't that mean *you* have the power?'

'The thing' being the blog? Of *course* it was the blog he wanted. And she wanted him to want *it* rather than her. And she *didn't* want him to think he could get it for peanuts… So, yes, she needed to act as if *she* had the power. As if she couldn't care less.

Overheating and unable to answer, Stephanie could only manage action. She shoved the phones into the glove compartment and closed it with a definite slam. Then she curled her fingers into empty fists. At home she worked on her laptop most of the time. To be completely disconnected from the internet felt weird. But to take up Jack Wolfe's challenge and beat him? Irresistible…

'What will you take as *your* prize?' he asked conversationally, his eyes back on the road.

Oh, she'd make him pay. 'Two hours' hard labour.'

She'd bet he'd never done a real job in his life—not even when he was volunteering during his 'do-good' year.

'Hard labour?' His gaze narrowed. 'Such as…?'

'Such as you shifting a pile of bricks from one side of a yard to another. And back again. For two hours. I'll watch to make sure you don't stop—not even for a minute.'

'That's kinda boring, don't you think? You'd get bored.'

Watching him work up a sweat? She didn't think she would, actually. 'No, I wouldn't.'

'Why?' He turned his head, and something dangerous burned in his expression. 'You like to look?'

Stephanie was unable to answer the heat in those eyes. Instead she reached into her small bag and pulled out her sunglasses, shoving them on and staring straight ahead. Hiding. And ignoring his soft, triumphant laughter.

Then she tried—*really* tried—to go totally 'Steffi Leigh'. For forty minutes or so she regaled him with a few of her favourite pre Dan's illness stories from when she'd first started vlogging. Jack listened, but didn't ask any more questions, didn't try to offer any topics of his own.

Eventually she fell silent, too tired to maintain the effort. As it was she'd lasted way longer than her usual two minutes. Besides, the further they got from the city, the more the tension drained away from her body, and it no longer seemed imperative that she somehow impress him with her blog's credibility every second. The sun warmed her…the wind on her face calmed her.

No phone. No internet. No contact. No care. Just a long stretch of road. And freedom.

She rested her elbow on the car door and rested her head on her hand, studying him from behind the dark lenses of her sunglasses. He turned to look at her, as if he were aware of her secret scrutiny.

He smiled.

It wasn't that wicked, teasing smile. Nor was it some polite *Are you doing okay?* kind of smile. It was genuine, intimate. And gorgeous.

The last block of tension within her crumbled. Her skin tingled and without thinking she smiled back—a mere curve of her lips. She didn't speak. There was nothing to say in that simple, perfect moment.

And slowly, as she basked in the warmth, her vision softened around the edges.

Vaguely she heard a low, muttered half-laugh. 'You *sure* there isn't something you want to run away from, fairy princess?'

She was too drowsy to bother answering. The plain truth was that she liked to look.

At him.

# CHAPTER FOUR

*THERE WAS NO LIGHT. She couldn't see him... She could only hear his cry for help, the sharp thump as he fell. He couldn't—wouldn't—get up, and she didn't have the strength to lift him on her own. And they were so alone.*

*'Dan, please...' She begged him to try. 'Please!'*

'Steffi?'

A deep, abrupt voice, right in her ear, yanked Stephanie from the darkness.

She sat up so quickly her seatbelt jerked and pulled her back against her seat with a *thwack*.

'You okay, there, sweetheart?'

Jack Wolfe was leaning over her, looking at her, his intense sky-blue eyes filled with concern and something she wasn't willing to name. He lifted his hand to her shoulder, holding her still so she didn't jump again. A calming, reassuring gesture. Only it made her heart thunder more.

She blinked, gazed into the deep blue of his eyes.

'Sleeping Beauty isn't supposed to have nightmares.'

He spoke quietly, but she heard the question in his tone.

Her wariness mounted as she wakened fully. What had she said? What was he thinking?

'I'm no Sleeping Beauty,' she muttered.

He sat back, giving her space, breaking the spell.

Good Lord, *how* had she fallen asleep? And how freaking *mortifying*. She was so embarrassed she didn't know what to say or where to look. Had she called out—given herself away? What else had she said or done? Snored? Drooled? Quickly she glanced down, checking her dress.

'Relax, princess, you look as perfect when you're sleeping as you do when you're awake.'

'You think I look *perfect*?' She tried to tease back, but she was too breathless and it came out all weak and woebegone and pathetic, embarrassing her even more.

'You know I do.'

She couldn't stop a small smile at that low-voiced growl. A glow of pleasure lit her up from the inside and eased the panicked pace of her pulse. She sneaked a glance at him.

He was smiling back at her—a small smile that barely broke through his seriousness. The curiosity in his gaze faded as another kind of emotion swirled and the heated intensity built, turning the atmosphere in the car sultry. She felt sucked into the centre of a burning bubble. Her brain rendered only one thought—*move closer*.

Uh… *No*. Bad idea.

She cleared her throat, embarrassment returning now she was wide awake and practically drooling over him. 'What time is it?'

'*Not* time to get your phone back!' He laughed. 'Relax. It's not midnight yet, so I don't think the car's about to turn into a pumpkin…'

'I'm no Cinderella either,' she said.

It wasn't that she had an evil stepmother—she had a brother counting on her. A vulnerable brother, dependent on her.

'Yeah, well, that's good—because I'm no Prince Charming.'

She quickly glanced at him again, caught the unmistakable meaning in his words. She understood—there might be attraction, but there was no 'happy-ever-after' to be had with him.

'No…you're missing the noble white steed.'

'Thank goodness. A horse would be *such* a hassle at

border control.' He sent her a sideways look. 'But don't get me wrong,' he whispered. 'I *love* to ride. Just not horses.'

She choked. He'd defused the moment—eased her embarrassment—with outrageous humour.

And, like her, the further they'd got from the city, the less burdened he'd become. Now that remote expression was gone, replaced with warmth and a smile.

'So this is it?' she asked, turning away from the dangerous proximity of him. 'We're here?'

Where *was* this so-fabulous hotel?

'Almost.' He restarted the engine and turned the steering wheel. 'I pulled over to wake you, so you wouldn't miss it.'

He gestured to the view ahead of them. She turned to look, drew breath as she finally registered that they were in the midst of a majestic forest.

Tall, tall trees that had to be hundreds of years old surrounded them. Trees and ferns and ancient woodland that made her feel insignificant, yet special at the same time. It was like a lost world. There was no sign of human habitation aside from the track they were now driving down.

'You're sure you're on the right road?' she asked.

'I'm sure.'

He drove for another ten minutes, taking them deeper into the forest. It felt as if they were miles from anywhere— as if they were entering a forbidden paradise. All trees and birds and isolation.

It was amazing.

'Beautiful, isn't it?' he asked.

She just nodded, because words simply didn't do it justice.

All of a sudden the road broadened, then ended in a wide circle. And at the apex a beautiful building had somehow materialised before them—a tall, two-storeyed, perfectly proportioned wooden palace.

The veranda that covered the deck, encircling it, was

painted a lush green that blended with the forest canopy.
The hotel was perfectly positioned to soak up the late-
afternoon summer sun, and even from the car she could see
it wasn't some rough-hewn, hippy-ish bed and breakfast.
The finish of the woodwork was perfect, and so finely detailed it had to have been built by master craftsmen.

It was like some sumptuous, treasure-filled hideaway
found in a 'journey-to-the-forbidden' fantasy movie.

'This is *amazing*. You'd never know it was here…' She
gazed up at it.

'Exactly. Which is why it provides such seclusion. Wait
'til you see the private swimming pool. And it's not far to
a lovely winery. Can't be all bad.'

All *bad*? It was all brilliant.

She turned to Jack, entranced by his sudden infectiously
buoyant mood. He walked round the front of the car and
then opened her door, leaning over it to smile at her.

'What do you think?'

Blinking, she forced herself to turn and look at the view
that for a moment had paled in comparison to the sight of
him.

She hadn't seen such a beautiful place. *Ever*. Not in the
photos her friends sent her to populate her blog with, not
on the internet, not in the movies.

She stepped out of the car and slowly followed him towards the steps.

'Don't you need to check in with someone?' Wouldn't
there be people around if this was a fancy hotel?

He turned and raised his brows at her.

'Like a receptionist or a concierge or something?' she
elaborated.

He chuckled and shook his head. 'The apartment is
open—they know I'm coming. And I've been here before,
so I know how it works.'

Had he brought a woman with him the last time he was here? She didn't want to know.

'This is an *apartment*?'

'Yeah, this entire building is ours for the night.'

Not for the night. Not for her.

'How…?' She narrowed her eyes. *How* had the hotel known he was coming tonight? Wasn't he earlier than planned? He'd been supposed to have a meeting with *her*…

But he was already climbing the stairs to that gorgeously ornate decking area.

'Come and see inside,' he called lazily.

Intrigued, she couldn't resist following. She paused in the doorway, blinking as her eyes adjusted to the dimmer light of the interior.

'Come on!' he teased.

The room wasn't huge, but the interior was cool and inviting. A luxurious rug covered part of the polished wooden floor. The walls were painted white. A large painting hung over the mantelpiece. She knew it wasn't a print but an original. Other art works adorned smaller spaces, and there was a sculpture displayed on a small plinth in one corner. Against the farthest wall there was a floor-to-ceiling bookcase—filled.

*So* pretty. So beautifully designed to draw her deeper and deeper into its delights.

There was a plush sofa, large enough for two to stretch out on, and two armchairs. And through the other door she could see the bedroom. All pure white linen, wooden bedframe and tranquillity.

'You can see the pool from this window,' he called to her, from the window by the sculpture.

She walked over and peered out.

The pool was a glorious green-blue, built to look like any natural pond to be found in the heart of that gorgeous forest. To the side of it there were a couple of items of furniture—but the one that caught her eye was a beautiful wicker four-poster daybed, its thick mattress and plump cushions clad also in pure white linen. White drapes hung on three sides to protect its occupants from the sun…and from prying eyes…

The romantic atmosphere couldn't be denied.

'This is a couples' retreat.' She glanced away, trying not to be impressed—or aroused. 'This is all massage and seclusion and…'

*Intimacy. Isolation.* And a really, *really* big bed. Two beds, in fact. One indoors. One out.

'Massage?' he queried, *not* innocently.

'Yeah—you can't tell me they don't do massages and facials and deep tissue rejuvenation and stuff.'

'You don't like massage?' he asked, his expression comically shocked. 'I'd have thought massages would be your jam.'

Her 'jam'? Oh, she didn't think so.

'They don't work.' She'd given her brother so many massages and they'd never helped *him*.

'You've not been getting the right massages.'

He walked ahead of her, right into the bedroom.

As she glanced about she saw a billion photo opportunities. If only she had a decent camera with her. But her phone was still out of bounds, in the glove compartment of the car.

She walked to the doorway and saw him standing near the bed. Her unruly imagination instantly flashed images of him *on* it—naked and aroused and hungry.

She backed out of the intimacy of the room, going on to the veranda that ran the entire circumference of the building. She only stopped when she felt a safe distance from that insanely erotic bedroom. She ignored the twin wicker chairs that were placed at close angles and instead leaned against the railing.

She tried not to stiffen when she heard his footsteps coming nearer a few moments later.

'If you're very careful, and very quiet, you might see one of your precious echidnas,' he said softly, dropping into the chair just behind her.

She turned to face him, leaning her elbows on the railing, refusing to let him see how much he—and this place—had got to her. Except the pose pulled her dress tight across her breasts, and they felt too full as it was. And she'd *totally* just given herself away by literally running from the bedroom.

'I thought you weren't that interested in animals?' she said weakly.

'Zoos, not so much,' he admitted, with a teasing lilt to his words. 'But who doesn't love little wild animals? I just prefer to see them in their native habitat rather than in some artificially created display where they're expected to perform. You can learn a lot about a creature by seeing its habitat.'

'Artificially created display'? Like her blog? He *so* wasn't hiding his implied meaning. Well, he wasn't seeing *her* native habitat.

He chuckled at her expression, reading her thoughts. 'Keep your secrets—I'll find them out eventually.'

'I don't have any secrets.'

She looked at the way he'd sprawled back in the elegant chair. It wasn't an entirely indolent pose. She had the impression he could move as fast as a cheetah if he chose.

'Everyone has secrets.'

Her blood chilled. So he suspected she was withholding something? Of course he did. He'd heard her calling out in her sleep.

She turned it back on him. 'Tell me one of yours.'

He held her gaze. 'I have a meeting two days from now

that I've been waiting for my whole life. But I'm dreading it.'

She gazed down at him, knowing he was telling the truth. A big truth. 'So which is the secret? That you're having the meeting or that you're dreading it?'

'Both.'

She was unable to look away and break the deepening intimacy of the moment. The memory of his stark expression earlier smote her heart.

'Who's the meeting with?' It *so* wasn't her business, but she couldn't stop herself asking.

'Nope—that's all you're getting. At least until you give me something.'

She wasn't giving him anything. Even though there was a weak part inside of her wanting to open up and let him in on her secret. She couldn't. He wouldn't want to buy the blog. And the blog—the sale of it—was the only reason she was here. It had to be.

'This would be a fantastic place for me to profile,' she said, snapping back into Steffi Leigh mode.

He eased further into the chair and smiled. 'What would be your angle?' He went along with her change of topic.

'Exclusivity, of course. It's obvious everywhere you look. This isn't for the average consumer. Only the super-rich could stay here. So I guess it's aspirational for those who want to *be* super-rich. A peek into how the other half live.' She glanced about at the decor. 'And I could pull together a list of some of the interior designs ideas you could borrow to create the same sanctuary effect in your own home.'

'You feel it's like a sanctuary?'

'Of course. Don't you?'

'It's quiet,' he acknowledged. 'I get lots of work done here.'

Was that why he'd come here—to have a couple of days' private preparation before whatever that meeting was?

She threw him a scornful look. 'You can't *work* here—it's like…sacrilegious or something.'

He chuckled. 'It's a good place to work.'

'The surroundings are serene, but it's the isolation that really gets you.' She nodded, stepped away from the railing. 'I ought to leave you in peace so you can indulge in it.'

He reached out, encircled her wrist with his hand. 'What if it isn't peace that I want to indulge in?'

She froze. Her eyes met his. She felt more snared by them than by his grip on her.

'What if I don't want to be alone tonight?' he added softly.

'Then you should have stayed in town,' she said huskily.

'Silly me.' He nodded. Not sounding at all sorry. 'If you stayed tonight I wouldn't be alone.'

She forced herself to swallow. 'I've already told you I'm not staying.'

'You're too tired to drive all that way back tonight. You couldn't even stay awake for the duration of the drive here,' he jeered softly, his fingers tightening ever so slightly. 'Stay the night.'

'That's not going to happen.' Somehow she had to defend herself against this seduction. Because that was what it was—an easy, intoxicating seduction. He wore his appeal so well. 'I'll drive back now.'

She couldn't possibly stay. Aside from the sheer wrongness of it, she had nothing with her. No clothes. No makeup. Nothing. And no Tara to put her look together. She didn't pay attention when Tara titivated her—she was usually dreaming up an intro or writing up another list. Sure, she knew the basics, but she couldn't achieve this level of 'blending' on her own. Steffi Leigh would disappear the second she dived into that pool…

'Can you even drive that car?' he asked, his eyes too keen and knowing.

'I don't find her *that* easy to handle,' she admitted. 'But I'll manage.'

He chuckled, but she felt it was at some private joke rather than at her words. 'I'll drive you back tomorrow.'

She shouldn't stay—couldn't, in fact—but somehow she found herself asking, 'Is there more than one bedroom?'

Slowly he released her wrist. 'What is it you think I'm offering?'

Oh, they *both* knew—he couldn't play coy now.

'You're the one making a bet with a kiss as the prize.'

His wicked smile flashed. 'There are two bedrooms. Two beds. We'll have to share a bathroom, though. Shall I show you?'

He rose from the chair. In a moment he was towering above her, and his size and proximity had an immediate devastating impact on her.

She tensed, waiting for him to move. It felt like for ever until he did.

He led her back through the lounge area and into the master bedroom. He stood aside, letting her walk through first this time, and gestured to the open doorway she'd not had time to notice earlier.

The bathroom was incredible. Where there ought to have been a wall there was a window that gave an unrestricted view of the lush trees. There was a flash of colour as a bird flew by.

It was like being in Eden. And just as full of temptation.

'The glass is specially tinted,' he commented. 'You can see out, but no one can see in. They just get the reflection of the forest...of themselves.'

She looked from him down to the huge, deep bath that stood between them. It had ample space to fit two adults.

She imagined that bath filled with warm water and

masses of bubbles. She'd sink into it and just luxuriate in it—soak for hours, gazing out at that beautiful green scene. And how nice would it be to have a man with her…to be enveloped in his embrace?

She hadn't soaked in a bath in such a long time. She hadn't been alone with a man in such a long time. She hadn't had anything for *her* in such a long time.

This whole place was a divine assault on her senses. Tempting every single one. And Jack Wolfe was pure temptation too.

She looked from that deep bath to him, and all her ability to resist the intimacy of the situation fled. The erotic undercurrents that had been bubbling all afternoon rose to the surface. She could almost *feel* steam building within the room as primal need blossomed—as pure want flowed through her.

Jack stood in the doorway, transfixed by the expression on her face. She looked as if she'd never before seen something so seductive or so decadent. Which totally didn't make sense. Hadn't he seen pictures of her various escapades? Didn't she talk up all the luxuries in town?

He glanced down at her legs. Beneath the prim hemline of her dress her skin looked pale—which was interesting, given she'd been talking about her amazing trip to New Zealand when he'd last skimmed her blog—swimming with dolphins and bungee-jumping had been listed in that post. But had she spent her time there staring at her computer screen, obsessing over her number of views, instead of staying in the water and playing in the sun?

He didn't really care, because her half-smile now was so genuine and so full of sensual promise. Her eyes were lit, gleaming blue-green. It was as if her 'blogalista' veneer had fallen away and she was complete—so much more than the façade she first presented. There was depth there now. And desire.

Desire that also ravaged through him.

He almost suggested that she strip out of her dress—that he'd run a bath for her there and then. He'd soap her...help her relax... But, while the sparks between them were undeniable, it was still too soon. She was skittish. Only minutes before she'd backed away. And he'd been stunned when she'd fallen asleep three-quarters of the way along the drive here. She'd looked vulnerable and sweet. Her make-up, her whole 'look', was a mask for her to hide behind. She wasn't anywhere near the confident confection she projected herself as being—hell, she'd cried out for help in her sleep.

The question was *why*.

Jack Wolfe knew when someone was holding something back—when they had something they didn't want to share. Eye contact faltered, conversation topics changed quickly... Yeah, he knew the hurt of having secrets withheld from him. His parents had held out on him for years. And even if it had been done for love—to protect him—it still hurt.

And it had hurt his ability to trust *anyone*.

He could make a quick call and get his PI to check her out—but he didn't want to, because he also knew how finding the truth in that way could hurt just as badly as not being told at all. He'd prefer she talked to him herself.

Okay, he wanted her to do something much more personal than *talk*.

So she had demons? Everyone did. Especially him. Right now talking about them wasn't what mattered—what mattered was getting away from them. And that was the one thing he and she could do together. They could have the most fantastic few hours of escape. And he ached for it.

From the moment he'd seen her, walking across that hotel foyer as cool as a cucumber and yet with those deeply expressive eyes, he'd been in her thrall. And right now she was looking at him as if she wanted him as much as he wanted her.

Utterly, passionately, inevitably.

'You hungry?' he asked.

'Pardon?'

Her voice sounded husky, and he saw that startled look enter her eyes.

He bit back a smile. Yeah, still skittish. But he'd get there. Like a hunter closing in on his pretty prey, he enjoyed the chase. The seduction. Because the need to conquer was so keen.

He didn't care about the call from Bella. The report he ought to be writing could wait. For once he wanted to push everything else to the side while he concentrated on taking this challenge of a woman to the limits of her sexual pleasure.

'Food,' he explained, in a word of one syllable, because that was all his overheated brain could manage. 'You want to eat?'

'I…don't…'

'Steak? Fish? Vegetables? Or does eating ruin your "look"?' Jack needled.

'I can't stay…' Her voice tailed away on a husky rasp.

Sure she could. And she *would*.

But for now he smiled, trying to pull back on the smouldering erotic embers threatening to flare up between them. 'You can't drive all that way back without decent sustenance. What can I order for you?'

The emerald in those gleaming eyes deepened. 'Surprise me.'

There was a charged silence while he fought to stay in control of his own damn libido.

'How do we order?' she asked huskily. 'Are we allowed to break out our phones?'

'You can make a call if you want—but you know what will happen.'

He watched her think about it, willed her to take up the challenge. To lose that stupid bet.

She hadn't figured out that he'd used his phone while she slept. He wouldn't tell her until she asked. He wanted to kiss her more than to own up right now. And he didn't care if that made him a jerk.

'There's an intercom system,' he explained finally. 'I'll go organise something.'

She nodded.

Ordering only took a couple of minutes, and he knew from experience that it wouldn't be long before the discreet staff served them.

'Why don't we have a drink on the veranda while we wait for the food to arrive?' he suggested. 'Champagne?'

She shook her head as she walked out to the deck. 'I won't drink alcohol—it's a long drive.'

She was afraid of losing her inhibitions with him. Was it because she was close to that already? His skin tightened. He liked the thought of her being as clear-headed as him when it came to it. It would make her surrender to him all the more satisfying. And he'd make damn sure *she* was satisfied.

'Juice?' he offered instead.

'That would be great.' She bit her lower lip. 'But don't let me stop you enjoying a drink.'

'I don't drink alcohol. My birth mother was an addict— I've no intention of making the same mistake.' Why he'd said it, he didn't really know. To shock her? To see if he could shake that perfect façade again?

Her eyes widened. 'I'm sorry about your mother,' she said softly.

'I'm addicted to travel instead,' he joked lightly, wanting to step back from that too personal admission.

'And work?' she noted.

'One and the same.' He smiled. 'My brothers lay into me all the time about being a workaholic. But George is such a party animal *anyone* would look like a workaholic compared to him.' He glanced at her. 'And you're addicted to the internet?'

'True,' she admitted. 'But some addictions are worse than others.'

'Maybe.' He shrugged as he went to the small discreet bar fridge and found the juice options. 'All can be damaging.'

'But some can help people build great things.'

'And others can destroy.' He poured two glasses of juice.

'So what about balance, then?' she asked.

'Impossible—we all know that.'

'So you're all or nothing?' she teased.

'I think so.'

He was all gorgeous. Stephanie took the glass he offered and went outside to sit in one of the wicker chairs. The sun was starting its slow descent, casting a gorgeous red-orange glow over the treetops and the smooth water. She'd barely had a chance to take a sip of her drink when she heard a vehicle pulling up.

'Give me a second...' He walked round the corner of the deck.

For a crazy moment she thought she might give him anything he asked for.

She collapsed back into the comfortable cushions as he walked from view. She *so* had to get a grip on herself. She did *not* run away with handsome men. Did *not* do whatever they suggested with no regard to anyone else. Her *mum* did that, but not Stephanie.

So she had to get out of here while she still could.

But then he reappeared, wheeling a sleek trolley towards

her, looking so fine in that white shirt and those navy trousers and with that edgy look back in his eyes.

'Silver service?' she asked, taking in the gleaming dishes. Quality simply dripped from every aspect of the place.

'You'd expect anything less?'

No. She wouldn't. And she imagined there'd be some unbelievably rich concoction on the trolley that she wasn't sure she could stomach.

He lifted the lids with a flourish and she found she was wrong. Her mouth watered when she saw the vibrant, juicy slices of fruit on the nearest tray.

'I get sick of plastic plane food when I'm travelling. And restaurant food can get too rich. Sometimes simple is perfect, right?'

He glanced at her.

She nodded in mute agreement. The platters were beautiful—fruits, cheeses, sliced meats, vegetables, creamy dips. Fresh and real and delicious.

'Finger food. You might have to take off your gloves,' he said.

Or she could recline, as in Roman times, and be fed grapes by a handsome attendant... And where had *that* thought come from?

'I wasn't lying about my nails.' Reluctantly she peeled off one glove, then the other.

'I never said you were.' He picked up her hand and looked down at her broken and chipped nails. 'You get nervous?'

He rubbed his thumb over her palm, stopping her from instinctively curling her fingers into a fist. She tried to quell the shiver that ran through her. And she tried to banish the image of him touching her in other more intimate places.

*Sex.*

She'd hardly had any in her life, and all of a sudden it was all she could think of. All she wanted.

'It's just a habit. I know it's gross.' She tugged her hand free, embarrassed that he'd seen how bad her nails were, and reached for a cooling slice of melon. 'I get false ones put on…but they come off… I just didn't have time to get them redone before this meeting.'

'Because you were so busy on your blog?'

She glanced at him and saw he wasn't being sarcastic. 'I'm always trying out the products, writing the content. Dreaming up yet more content.'

'It must be hard to come up with lots of content all the time.'

She paused, not taking a bite of the melon. Did he suspect her? Did he know the truth? That she got as much as possible from her old schoolfriends. The trouble was, the busier they got the less they sent to her. She lived vicariously as they texted her pictures from their parties at the coolest new venues. And all the meals she posted about on her blog? Texted to her by Tara, or some of the other friends who'd stuck by her since school.

She was a total fraud.

'I ought to take a couple of photos,' she said, glancing back into the gorgeous room.

'That would mean using your phone,' he pointed out, then laughed at her expression. 'One day without an update isn't going to matter, is it? Anyway, I'm betting you have a week's worth preloaded, right? With the odd gap for something ultra-current? No one is going to know you've run away for a night. You're in the clear.'

'You understand the process well.' She chose to ignore the bit about running away for the night. And to ignore the whisper of want within her urging her to agree.

'It's my business to. We've been watching your blog for a while.'

'Enjoying the tips?'

'Enjoying watching your numbers grow. You've struck a chord with a segment of the market that we'd like to tap into. We'd like to take your success and replicate it.'

She wasn't sure big business could create the same kind of in-your-own-home feel. But she wasn't about to argue with him.

'What's on the other side of the camera?' he asked. 'Your vlogs are always filmed in the same space. Why don't you go into another room?'

'It's what people have come to expect. The format... the habit.'

'But how do you keep it fresh?'

'With the content within the framework. I love tweaking, and the content is always changing.'

'While you always present the perfect façade?'

She stiffened inside at that faint hint of disapproval. 'It's what people expect. It's part of what they're looking for.'

'And you don't think they'd stick around if they saw the bitten-down nails? What's wrong with a little reality?'

'Nothing.' She smiled. 'But my site is about *escape*.'

'You said you had nothing to escape from?'

She couldn't answer that. So she opted for diversion. 'Tell me about this weird fruit—do you know what it is?' she asked.

He frowned slightly, but followed her lead.

The rest of the meal they spent sparring lightly on topics she deemed safe. But inside her anxiety was rising again. She had to leave. She needed to ensure Dan was okay—that Tara had seen him and made sure of it. He ought to be well asleep by the time she got home, but she didn't want to be worrying about him the entire drive back.

So while Jack went to contact the invisible hotel aides to get them to collect the trolley she quickly tiptoed down the stairs to where the car was parked. She reached into the glove compartment and quickly pulled out her phone.

There were no more messages, so she quickly texted Tara.

I'm going to be even later. Please check Dan and let me know he's okay. Text asap.

She waited a moment, watching to ensure that the text was sent—there wasn't great coverage here. But she had a reply less than a minute later.

Be as long as you like. All good here. Go be bad.

Fantastic. But she wasn't going to be bad—merely late.

She switched off her phone and turned to put it back into the glove compartment before Jack caught her. But as she closed the compartment she heard footsteps behind her.

'You couldn't resist, could you?' He walked up to where she'd frozen by the side of the car. 'You made a call?'

She straightened and turned defensively. 'Extenuating circumstances.'

'No.' He took two steps closer, so he was towering over her. Captivating her. 'We had a bet. You lost. I win.' He smiled. 'But we both know you win too.'

'Oh? I should consider myself *lucky*?' She rolled her eyes, but couldn't hide her breathiness. 'You're so arrogant you probably think I used it deliberately.'

'Didn't you?'

'It was unavoidable.' And unexplainable. She'd had to check on Dan. She couldn't *not*.

'You can tell yourself that if it makes you feel better.' He put his hands on his hips and stood with his feet planted wide, as if ready to block any attempt she might make to escape. 'Time to pay up, fairy princess.'

'You can't be serious?' And she was not *any* kind of princess—certainly not fairy.

'Sure I can.'

Yeah, she knew that seriousness was his default setting—that the flashes of wicked humour came only when he was relaxed, with his mind taken off whatever it was worrying him. Whatever that meeting was about.

She tried one last time. 'This is inappropriate.'

'Yeah, but we had an agreement.'

She closed her mouth, biting back the words because the more she said, the more determined he seemed to become.

So she'd take it—be unmoved. And walk away.

Primly she waited, tilted her chin back as he neared. She wasn't going to make it difficult for him. Or easy.

That hard-edged hungry look sharpened his features... desire glinted in his eyes. Part of her wanted to run far and fast. Another part wanted to press closer to him—and not just her lips. She wasn't sure which urge was most dominant.

Now he'd got to within kissing distance.

She held her breath. Couldn't move. Anticipation slithered through her like mercury dancing up a thermometer on a burning hot day.

Only now he hesitated. She saw his expression alter as he looked down to her mouth, then back up to her eyes. A muscle ticked in his jaw as he seemed to be thinking something through.

All she could do was look up at him, waiting, *willing*.

For a moment she thought he was going to walk away without doing anything. But then, very gently, he lowered his head, keeping his tense body a clear five inches from hers. He merely brushed his lips on her cheekbone. A little too close to her ear, and for a little too long to be totally brotherly, but it wasn't the hot, dominant, French kiss that she'd expected.

That she'd *wanted*.

As he pulled back to study her face, disappointment swamped her. *That was it?*

'Wow…' she said dryly. But she stepped back to lean against the car because, despite the total chasteness of that 'kiss', her legs felt wobbly. And, given the sudden flare of heat in his eyes, he'd seen her real reaction—her disappointment. She tried to cover up with sarcasm. 'You just blew my mind.'

'I know.' He laughed softly, but then fell silent.

She stared back up at him, feeling almost baleful. All that anticipation… All that teasing… He hadn't meant it.

'I'll kiss you properly if you really want me to.'

A steely whisper in the hot, sultry night. A taut wire of promise. He was watching her closely.

What had made him think she *didn't* want him to?

He stood stock still as he waited for her answer. His gaze sharpened.

'Stephanie?' He angled his head, as if he was listening for something almost inaudible. 'You *want* me to kiss you properly?'

# CHAPTER FIVE

How could he not already know the answer? Stephanie frowned up at him, trying to figure out why he was hesitating when desire blistered the air between them.

He wanted to kiss her. He'd made that stupid bet especially. And he'd won it. But when it had come to claiming his prize he'd held back. Why?

Because he only wanted to kiss her that way if he had her full permission? Her full participation?

Well, for that the guy was going to have to be rewarded.

She couldn't help a small smile as she basked in his hot glare—in this overwhelming attraction. For real, right now, and—for her—so *rare*.

How could she *not* make the most of it? Just this once…

'Do I want you to kiss me *properly*?' she echoed, flawlessly Steffi Leigh.

He tensed even more—impossible though that seemed.

Stretching up onto her tiptoes, she focused on his mouth. She revelled in that moment of anticipation before she gave him the answer they both already knew.

'*Duh,*' she jeered.

She heard his little laugh, saw his movement—but she moved faster. In a heartbeat she'd pressed her lips to his.

And that was the only heartbeat in which *she* held the control.

His arms clamped around her and he hauled her closer. Then closer still—as if he couldn't get near enough to her. As if he'd been aching for total touch the way she had. Breast to chest, stomach to abs, hips to hardness, and *lips to lips.* His mouth moved over hers in a caress that segued quickly into a *claiming.* Absolutely the way she'd wanted to be kissed. Bold and sensual and consuming.

She'd closed her eyes, but the brilliant light from the evening sky burned on her retinas. It was such a beautiful place. She'd eaten such divine food. She was being seduced by more than the man himself, right? It was the whole deal. And she'd indulge in it—take this one moment to escape.

Because she was under no illusions. It wasn't that Jack had fallen for her or anything. Not after one afternoon. This was an escape for him too. Only she didn't know from what.

All she knew was that he wanted her the way she wanted him.

*Utterly. Now.*

Her bones melted, her muscles warmed, inhibition fled as his passion spun its magic. She felt so wanted. So needed. She drowned in the sensations, her head falling back as she let him take her weight, wholly drawn into his embrace.

Thoughts, worries, words dissolved along with any last hesitation as she swooned, seeking the heat and strength of him. His hands pulled her closer still. One stroked from her waist up her spine, pressing her stomach to his hard abs, the other shaped the curve of her butt.

She tingled everywhere they touched and felt the buzzing to her toes. The hunger for more deepened. She threaded her hands through his hair, holding him as tightly as he held her, holding his lips to hers. She couldn't get enough of him—so big, so strong, so *hot.*

In the blink of an eye she was ready to agree to anything—ready to demand. Burning up, she yearned to be naked.

His kisses lengthened, intensified, kinked. His tongue worked wicked sensual magic. She mewled when he stroked the roof of her mouth, when he swirled deeper.

So *not* chaste. So hot. So good.

Breathless now, she clung to him with both lips and hands, holding him so he could take more from her. Give her more.

Kiss after kiss after kiss.

'Stephanie...' he muttered suddenly.

She wasn't sure if it was a warning or a caress. She didn't care. She just wanted more kisses. More everything.

He groaned against her and pulled back. 'This is...' he breathed out harshly '...crazy.'

Not the word she'd have chosen. Not what she wanted to hear. She wanted to hear only groans, sighs. She wanted to dive again into those bottomless pools of sensation, of touch and taste. She wanted to feel his hot, hard strength against her, pushing her towards ecstasy. Right now she wanted it all, wanted to reach oblivion.

Just for once.

'Stephanie?'

He gently shook her in his arms. Belatedly she realised she'd been leaning against him breathlessly, like a heaving-bosomed heroine in a period drama. Only she couldn't blame her breathlessness on a too tight corset. It was all him.

Now a droplet of ice ran the length of her spine and she made herself open her eyes.

He'd tensed, but to her relief that inferno was still within him. He was gazing down at her with that ravaging hungry look. Her toes curled in her kitten-heeled shoes.

'This is a bad idea,' he said.

But even as he spoke he swept his hand from the small of her back over the curve of her butt, pulling her hips flush to his again. His erection rammed against her belly.

She trembled at the touch. Relieved, craving.

'Yes.'

He frowned. 'But I want to—'

'Yes.'

He shook his head at her interruption, and a wisp of a smile crossed his face before frustration edged it out. 'You don't understand. I want to do…*everything.*'

'Yeah, I'd kind of guessed that from your body language…' She let her words trail, rocked her pelvis against his.

His hand on her butt tightened. His lips quirked again. 'Cute. But—' He broke off to frown again. 'I don't want *complicated.*'

'That's fine—because I don't do complicated,' she muttered.

In truth, she didn't do *anything.* Boyfriends hadn't been forthcoming since Dan's illness. Truth be told, they hadn't been forthcoming prior to that trip either. After her one flop of a relationship she'd chosen to focus on other things. Now it had been so long since she'd had sex she wasn't sure she could remember how. All she knew was that she didn't want this moment to end—not yet. What harm were a few kisses? Maybe a little more? Maybe everything if they so wanted. Okay, *she* so wanted.

Just quickly. Just once. Just *now.*

He gazed at her. She could see him thinking, wavering, deciding.

'While we're here we don't talk work,' he said, suddenly brusque. 'Not here. Not now. Not tonight.'

'Fine.' She nodded, running her tongue over her dried lips. 'No work talk 'til Melbourne.'

She'd not expected him to offer her a deal at this first meeting anyway. And truthfully she didn't want to have to be 'Steffi Leigh' right now. She just wanted to indulge.

'This…excursion…is off the record. For both of us. I won't let this affect any decision I take on your blog, okay?'

He still looked too serious for her liking.

'We can keep it simple?' he asked.

Like she hadn't got it already? 'I'm not stupid,' she groaned.

'Yeah, but we need to know we stand with each other.' His hand pressed on her curves again, letting her know *exactly* how he was standing.

'Let me see if I can figure it out,' she drawled. 'You come—you go. Right?'

'Right.' He nodded slowly, a rueful expression entering his eyes.

'But in this case I'll be the one going.' She smiled guilelessly. And that was good. She could indulge this once in passion but do no harm. There was no threat of an all-consuming affair in which she'd lose her soul.

He studied her for a heated moment, then swiftly bent and kissed her.

'You're not going until you've come,' he muttered against her lips. 'I want to see you come.' He stepped forward, pressing more tightly against her. 'I want to taste you when you come.'

Heat ricocheted round her body. *That* was what he wanted to do? Uh…sure. She was okay with that.

Her breathing quickened. Anticipation tautened her nerves. It was crazy that she had that much reaction to only a hint of dirty talk. But the promise he conveyed with just a look…

She snatched a couple of deep breaths. Such mesmerising sexual attraction was a little scary.

But she'd had a moment to think and, while she wanted this moment, she needed to keep things in perspective. She couldn't—wouldn't—forget her responsibilities.

She framed his face with her hands and looked into his eyes so she knew she had his attention. 'Ten minutes, then I'll leave.'

He swiftly turned his head and kissed her palm, before looking back into her face. Amusement danced in his eyes. 'Ten minutes?' He couldn't hold back the laugh. 'You're kidding, right?'

'No.' She knew it wasn't going to take half that time for her to come—not if he set his mind to it. 'I have to get going,' she explained.

'Why? Who's waiting for you?'

'No one,' she breathed, goosebumps feathering her skin at the lie. 'I just…have to get back to the city…'

'Tara will feed your cat…stay the night.'

Before she could answer he kissed her, sending her straight back into that sensual haze.

Every cell in her body tingled and sought movement, sought to get nearer to the source of that heat. Never had she felt this kind of attraction. Never had she taken this kind of pleasure in something as simple as touch.

'I have to go.' Breathless, she struggled to make him understand. To make herself stick to her own rule. 'Ten minutes.'

He swept both hands down her back to cup her bottom. Holding her close, he thrust against her. Caught by surprise, she clutched his shoulders and rode the wave, almost coming on the spot.

His laugh was low and sexy and full of wicked promise. 'Then I guess I have ten minutes to change your mind.'

He kept his hands in place and lifted her—too easily. He took a couple of steps and then set her onto the bonnet of the car, pushing her back so she lay down. Of their own accord her legs splayed wide, leaving space for him to fill. He took it. The metal against her back and butt was warm from the sun, but the real heat now leaned over her. Against her.

She couldn't hold back the moan as she felt part of his weight on her. Maybe it was madness, but never had she been so lost to lust. Never had she craved contact in such a raw way. She couldn't hold her hips from their instinctive arch towards him as he braced above her. Framed by that brilliant blue sky, he was truly the sexiest man she'd ever seen. And the way he was looking at her…

'Ten minutes,' he said softly.

Then there were no more words. There were kisses. And there were touches too. And thank goodness she was on her back and no longer having to stand, because she simply wouldn't be able to—not when he was skimming his palm down the side of her waist like that—not when he was pressing kisses across her collarbones—not when his fingers were toying with the hem of her dress, teasing underneath it to stroke her thighs before skittering back down. And then starting again. Every time going higher beneath her skirt. Going lower towards her neckline. Kissing more skin…uncovering more of her body.

She arched again, seeking more, unable to stop her innate need to draw him closer. The heat was burning her inside out. *She* wanted everything.

Finally he returned to her mouth, kissing her deep and lush. Then he lifted his head. Bracing on his elbows, he caught her eyes and then rolled his hips—pressing his erection against her.

'Stay the night.'

'I can't…' She shuddered, almost devastated.

It had only been five minutes—tops. All she needed was another kiss, another touch, and she'd be *there*. That would do. That was all she wanted now—just to come. And for him to come. She wanted to *feel* him.

He kissed her again. Thrust against her again.

'Stay the night. The whole damned night. With *me*.'

He didn't give her the chance to deny him again. Instead he kissed her endlessly, making it impossible for her to answer anything. Making it impossible for her to *think*.

His hands resumed their playful skimming beneath her skirt—only this time they went higher, then higher still. He shifted slightly, easing the way he was pressed against her.

And then she felt his fingers gently stroking at the edge of her panties. She gasped as he kissed her, then groaned as those skilful fingers breached the fabric barrier.

Skin on skin. Firm touches on slick heat. Slipping into searing intimacy. Gentle, rhythmic, maddening. And not enough. *So* not enough.

She groaned into his kiss, winding her arms more tightly around his neck, mentally *begging* him not to stop.

He lifted his mouth from hers again.

'I'll drive you back first thing in the morning,' he promised. 'You'll have all day to work if you have to. Stay with me now.'

She shook her head but at the same time rocked her hips—grinding herself against his hand, seeking just a couple more strokes of his fingers.

She wanted to come.

'Stay. The. Night.' He punctuated the demand with kisses—starting at her throat then going lower, to her cleavage.

Her bra was too tight. She was too hot. She wanted to be naked.

He swiftly pulled away completely, and she gasped in disappointment. But before she could speak he lifted her skirt to her waist, baring her legs to the heat of the sun—and to his even hotter scrutiny. She squeezed her innermost muscles in instinctive response to his hungry, determined look. Slowly his lashes lifted as he looked from the tops of her thighs to her breasts, to her face.

Holding her gaze in his, he gently fingered the elastic of her panties again. She stopped breathing. He grasped the fabric in his fist and tugged. She arched again, enabling his movement so her panties slid down. He bent to kiss a couple of places on her legs as he pushed her panties right off.

'I've been imagining you like this all day,' he muttered. 'Warm and wet and spread wide for me.'

And now she was wetter.

'Jack…' She swallowed.

'Stay the night.'

She shook her head slightly, couldn't even voice the denial now.

He smiled. It wasn't a gentle smile.

She shivered, realising just how single-minded he was. His hand skimmed up the inside of her thigh again. *Yes.* She wanted those fingers back, wanted that rhythm.

But it wasn't his fingers that touched her this time. Her breathing shortened as he kissed her thighs, slowly working his way up. He stopped just short. And she gasped.

He hooked her legs over his shoulders, slid his hand firmly beneath her, tilting her so she was open to him.

She cried out at the first lick. So abandoned. So lost to the pleasure.

'Please…' she said as he paused.

She'd never had any kind of sex like this—not outdoors. Not so intimate. Not within a few hours of meeting a man.

'You want me to make you sing?' he asked, his voice like gravel.

'Make me scream,' she whispered, closing her eyes against the blinding brilliance of the sinking sun.

She felt him flinch. Felt his hand on her butt tighten.

He bent over her, kissing her. His tongue teased her sensitive spot in wicked circles, then quick flicks. His fingers teased too, tracing a pattern up and down her inner thigh, coming so close to where she wanted him to touch again. To complete her. Making her want him so much that she was arched and clawing at his shoulders.

And it was then that he paused. Once more determination brightened the blue in his eyes.

'Stay the night. Say yes.'

She realised his plan. He wasn't going to let her come until she'd answered him.

She gazed down to where he hovered just above her. So focused. So intent on her pleasure. And something within her snapped.

Why *shouldn't* she have one night just for her? Just this once? What consequences could there be? How could one night hurt? It wasn't as if she was going to up and leave for good.

His expression changed and he shifted his hand up her thigh.

Somehow he knew.

'Stephanie?' He slid his finger inside her.

'Yes…' She sighed in pleasure.

'You'll stay the night,' he said.

No longer a question. No longer needing an answer.

He fixed his mouth to her, drawing that sensitive nub deep into his hot mouth and flicking his tongue.

'Oh, *yes*,' she sobbed, her mind lost as he sucked her into orgasm.

It hit so quickly, so intensely, she screamed. Her hands tightened in his hair, her toes curled, her muscles quivered. The bliss coursing along every nerve-ending was so good she almost couldn't cope.

So good she never wanted it to end.

But it did. As the spasms ebbed he shifted, still pressing against her, slipping his arms beneath her back to cushion her against the hot metal of the car and waiting while she caught her breath. She could feel him ever so gently rocking against her—enough to keep her arousal near, to keep the aftershocks rippling through her.

So delicious. They were so *not* done.

'Finish it,' she whispered. She wanted to feel him inside her. 'Please.'

'Not yet. Not now I have all night,' he murmured in answer. 'I want to taste you some more first.' He kissed her deeply. 'You taste good.'

She trembled in his arms and wound her own more tightly against him, wriggling beneath him as she did so. She ached to feel him within her.

'So passionate,' he murmured. 'I knew it would be like this with you.'

Did he? Since when?

And now her brain clicked on. Dazed, she tried to absorb the fact that within two minutes of him kissing her she'd been willing to let him do anything and everything to her. It was shocking.

And she'd wanted to do it all to him.

She still did.

'You're staying,' he said.

He kept hold of her hand and pulled her to her feet.

She nodded and quickly pushed her skirt down. 'But I need to make a call.'

She turned away from him, tugging to free her hand. He wouldn't let her go. Instead he tugged right back, turning her to face him again.

He cupped her face with his other hand—feeling the heat of her cheek with his palm. 'You're embarrassed?'

She hated the concern that had sprung to his eyes. 'I don't normally behave this way,' she mumbled. *Too honest.* But she couldn't not be honest in this moment. Not after what they'd just shared—what he'd given her.

There was a moment's silence.

'Well, you should,' he said simply. 'And you shouldn't be embarrassed.'

He bent and picked her panties up from the ground, shoving them into his pocket.

How could she not be embarrassed *now*?

He straightened and held out his hand. 'Let's go inside.'

As she put her hand in his she saw his sudden smile. In a second—she had no idea how—he'd scooped her into his arms.

'You're going to carry me up all those stairs?'

'I have energy to burn.'

He was actually jogging?

'Don't waste it on this.' She was only half joking.

'Holding you close could never be a waste of energy.'

'Oh, *now* you're charming?'

'I'm always charming,' he countered.

She laughed. So *not*.

He swiftly climbed the stairs, then went straight through the bedroom and into the bathroom and set her on her feet.

'What are you doing?' She leaned back against the wall, her body still too tingly. Too needy.

'I saw the look on your face when you first saw this bath.' He flicked on the taps. 'I want to see you enjoy it.'

She wanted to enjoy *him* more first.

He chuckled as he walked towards her. 'The thing about staying the night is that now you have the time to enjoy it *all*.'

Yeah, but she still had *priorities*.

'You want more of me?' he teased, pulling her to lean against him again.

'Arrogant much?' she tried to tease back. But she *did* want more. And he knew it.

As he kissed her his hands worked on the zip of her dress. She wriggled her arms free so he could slide the fabric from her. Then she stood clad only in her white bra and kitten heels. No panties.

He stepped back and gazed down at her. 'Every inch is perfection, isn't it?'

Hearing a slight edge in his words, she felt the need for some Steffi Leigh protection. 'You're surprised?'

He glanced up. 'No.' His expression softened. 'Can I undo your hair?'

'You've undone everything else about me...' she muttered, half rueful now.

He shook his head. 'Not really. Not yet. I want to see you dishevelled. All messed up and sweaty.'

Hadn't he already? She'd been on her back with her legs spread and her naked butt hanging out for all the world to see while he sucked her. Now her face flamed at the recollection, while between her thighs her body slicked, readying again.

'You don't *want* me to see you messy?' His eyes narrowed as he misinterpreted the reason for the colour surging into her face. 'That just makes me want to do it more.' He laughed as he leaned close. 'You might like it.'

'Then do your worst,' she invited in a Steffi Leigh coo. 'Make me sweat.'

She stood still as he walked behind her. Very slowly, carefully, he removed the pins from her hair. She felt it loosening, then he ran his fingers the length of it as he freed it.

'It's longer than I realised. And more red,' he muttered—a sultry whisper in her ear as he gently massaged the nape of her neck. 'I've wanted to do this all afternoon.'

Just as he'd wanted to see her wet and ready for him?

'What else was on your mental checklist?' she asked, trying to sound cool, but now her voice was too wavery to pull it off.

'You're the one with the lists,' he teased. 'What's on *your* list?'

So *many* things. All which required him to be naked. Which he still wasn't.

He moved, switching off the bath taps, then turned back to her. Another kiss, and a movement as he unclasped her bra.

'Smooth…' she murmured.

'You haven't seen anything yet,' he drawled, then dropped to kneel at her feet. Carefully he removed one shoe, then the other.

'You're treating me like a princess,' she said as he picked her up again.

'That's a *bad* thing?' he teased, and lowered her into the water.

It lapped over her body, so warm and smelling so good, every bit as deep and luxurious as she'd imagined it would be. But how could she truly appreciate it when there was something else she wanted more?

He stood back, hands on hips, watching her.

'You're not going to join me?' she asked, almost ready to pout.

The bath was plenty big enough for two. And if it wasn't she could cope with going doubledecker. A thought which would have shocked her if she'd been able to think beyond this want. For someone not that experienced, she'd lost all inhibition quickly.

'Not this time,' he answered with a choked laugh. But he stepped forward and braced himself over the bath to look down at her. 'Is it as good as you thought it'd be?'

'I can't concentrate on the view of the forest when you're standing over me like that,' she said. 'And I'm in the mood to touch, not to look.'

She twisted her fist into the front of his shirt and pulled. Heard his laugh and then the splash as he half tumbled in. But the best thing was the slam of his body into hers.

She didn't care if he was half drowning her. He was *with* her, and that was what she wanted.

'Kiss me,' she demanded. 'And get naked.'

'So finally we get to your list?' he teased, kissing her.

'It's not a very long list,' she admitted.

She loved the feel of her wet, naked body pressing against his. She'd no doubt ruined his suit, but she didn't care.

Somehow his feet had found the floor again and he pulled away from her. 'Not yet,' he said.

'You're kidding?'

He knelt beside the bath, his fingers trailing in the water, making ripples around her. 'Shall I help you with the soap?'

'Oh…' Anticipation trickled through her. 'If you'd like.'

'Oh…' he echoed with a mocking inflection. 'I'd *like*.'

He started with her shoulders, her back, but it wasn't long before he sought out curves and secret spaces. It wasn't long before she was hot and eager.

'So responsive,' he muttered, leaning further into the bath to press kisses to her wet skin, to delve deeper below the surface.

'I've never… I don't usually…' She gulped for air.

'Physical attraction happens,' he soothed. 'Plus, you make me laugh.'

'I've discovered my life's meaning,' she drawled, to cover her embarrassment.

He chuckled. 'Exactly. And I've discovered mine.'

'What's that?'

'Making you hot. Making you want it so much you can't speak.'

'Making me want what?'

'Me.' His eyes glittered. 'Just…me.'

And he proceeded to do it. With only fingers, mouth and his full attention he had her wanting so much she could no longer stay still. No longer even *float*.

The water lapped over the edge of the bath, soaking him. He laughed softly as she whispered to him, begging him not to stop, begging him to join her. Begging him to take her. But he didn't. He just kept up the torture, wringing another orgasm from her.

She sank under the water to escape him for a second— to escape the intensity, to rally so she could fight back.

She might not be all that experienced, but she knew two-nil was not a good tally on the scoresheet. It was time to even things up a bit.

'I *really* think it's time you got naked,' she breathed.

Though he did the wet shirt look really, *really* well.

'In time.'

'No.' She stood up in the bath and stepped out of it with as much dignity as she could muster. *'Now.'*

She walked out of the bathroom without a backward glance. But her heart was beating crazily, and she was hoping that he'd let her take the lead this once and follow her.

She walked into the bedroom. That huge bed was magnificent.

She couldn't believe she was in such a place, with such a man.

Pure fantasy.

She suddenly froze and whirled to face him. 'Shouldn't you be staying back in Melbourne tonight? At the Raeburn?'

He nodded, smiling wryly. 'I was booked to stay here *tomorrow* night.'

'So when did you contact them to let them know you were arriving a day early? *And* with a guest?'

Because hadn't they put their phones in the glove compartment and made a bet not to use them?

He didn't answer. But his guilty expression couldn't be hidden.

'You *called* them.' She struggled to work it out. 'When I was asleep in the car.' Her eyes narrowed. 'You *cheated*.' She couldn't believe it. 'Now you owe me, you realise?'

'I do,' he conceded, without looking remotely apologetic. 'And I *was* going to confess.'

'When?'

'When the time was right.'

'Like next century?'

'Like the second I remembered what you'd asked for.' Her muscles thrummed.

'Two hours' hard labour.' He sent her a smouldering look

and started to unbutton his sopping shirt. 'How would you like me to pay up?'

There was a beat. The air seemed to be sweltering, making it impossible for her to breathe. To get badly needed oxygen to her brain. To *think*. Except she didn't want to think any more. She wanted only to *feel*. To enjoy this *escape*.

'You know already.'

This was why he'd been so keen to ensure her pleasure. To make her say yes and yes and yes again.

'Tell me.' He shrugged off the shirt and started on his trousers.

She couldn't.

'Did you want me to kiss you some more?'

Slowly she nodded. 'I want you to work very...*hard*.'

'I will do all the work. And I'm already hard. I've been hard since the second I first saw you.'

'You looked like you hated me.'

'No.' He kicked his trousers off. 'I didn't want to want you.'

'Why not?'

'I had...other things on my mind.'

'What's on your mind now?'

'Nothing but you.'

'This is why you brought me here? You decided back then?'

He frowned. 'I didn't bring you here expressly to—'

'Didn't you?' she challenged huskily. 'Am I not here to distract you? To be your entertainment?'

Something flashed in his eyes. 'Actually, I want to entertain *you*.'

'Oh, that makes *everything* okay, then.'

'I *will* please you. For more than two hours. For all the night.'

'Show me how you plan to do that.'

He smiled a promising smile that was more than a touch

wicked. 'I'll satisfy you until you can't scream a second longer.'

'Then you'd better get on with it.'

She walked to the bed and climbed onto it, stretching out in the very middle of the wide, white expanse. Her heart hammered as she watched him divest himself of the last of his clothing. Then, fully naked and arrestingly handsome, he walked about the room, taking the time to light a couple of the candles that had been placed in discreet corners. The scent was fresh and subtle. With no hesitation he opened a drawer and pulled out a box of condoms.

Stephanie's mouth dried as she watched him sheath his rigid length. She could only watch, awed at the beauty of him.

The candles were perfectly positioned to reveal the shadows and angles of his hewn body. The ache inside her intensified. Despite those two orgasms, she had more energy pent up in her body than ever.

Strong and hungry—she wanted his total touch. She wanted to feel him flush against her—bared, bucking against her. *Into* her.

She let herself fall into sensuality. Not caring about anything but gleaning every last drop of pleasure to be had with him this one night.

He paused to gaze at her. 'You're beautiful.'

Wordless, she shook her head slightly. 'It's the make-up.'

'It's your eyes—not what's painted on their lids. Anyway, the make-up is...' He chuckled. 'Smudged.'

'I have *panda eyes*?' she mock shrieked. 'Is that what you're telling me? And that's *beautiful*? You want to bonk a *bear*?'

He threw back his head and laughed.

She went to move, only he grabbed her and stopped her, falling with her back onto the bed. In that instant she no longer cared about her looks, only about what she was feeling.

'No, don't move—don't spoil it. Let me…' With his thumbs he wiped gently under each eye, then held them up to show her the faintest marks of black. 'Not so panda, really.'

That there was humour in this intensity just made her want him more.

He trailed his fingertips down her arms, following the movement with a hot gaze. She knew that he, like her, was willing to lose himself in touch. In sensation. To make the most of this moment. It was only about physical delight and satisfaction.

There would be only this. Nothing beyond. No repercussions. Only the decadence of *now*. And there was no room to dwell on anything but the sheer perfection of pleasure.

The mattress was depressed slightly as he knelt over her. She shimmied down, reaching out with her arms. There was only this simplicity now. Only this connection. The glorious freedom to touch—to taste. To take her pleasure in him.

And she did. Sweeping her widespread hands over his skin, drawing him closer, kissing every available part of him. Until he growled and rolled, pinning her. Placing her just were he wanted.

Where *she* wanted.

She gasped as he entered her with a fierce, sudden thrust. Closing her eyes to absorb the ferocity of the pleasure engulfing her, she moaned. Breathless, uncontrollable moans of overwhelmed delight.

'Tight…' He too sucked in a breath. 'You okay?'

*Oh…* She couldn't think enough to answer him…could only feel. And it felt so good.

'Stephanie?'

The edge to his tone penetrated her sensual fog.

'It's been a while…' She couldn't bear to meet his eyes. It had been *so* long. And in truth there'd only been the once, with the one man. And it hadn't been very good. She'd never lost herself like this. She stilled, embarrassed. 'Sorry.'

'Don't be sorry.' He half groaned, his breath hissing between his clenched teeth. 'You sure I'm not hurting you?'

'No… So good…' She muttered half-sentences in reassurance. 'Feel fantastic…'

She shifted her hips—only a tiny amount, because she was so full and he was so heavy. But she ached for him to move.

'Look at me,' he growled.

She opened her eyes, looked into his eyes. So close. So handsome.

He was braced on his elbows, taking a long look right back at her. Right into eyes. As if he could see into her aching soul. 'Stephanie.'

Now she *liked* it that he called her by her full name. That he didn't see her as Steffi Leigh.

'Please…' She bit her lip as a tremor of sensation took her by surprise. 'Don't hold back.'

Still he hesitated.

'I want everything,' she assured him. Then begged, 'Please.'

'I'll do anything if you ask me like that,' he groaned.

He kissed her. She sank into it as soon as his lips caressed hers.

He slid his hands beneath her, drawing her closer. She widened her legs, wrapping one around him, curling her arms around him too, so they were in the ultimate lovers' embrace.

Finally he moved, rocking deep into her. On pure instinct she met him stroke for stroke. There was a need she recognised in him that called to something within her. A desperate need for solace in sex.

To run away? To escape?

*Yes, please.*

'More.' She clutched his shoulders, moaning as she writhed beneath him as best she could, fighting to get the faster friction she suddenly knew she needed. That she knew *he* needed.

She was so close to coming, and she wanted to, but she wanted to crest that wave *with* him this time.

And he was close too. She could feel it in his body, see it in his eyes.

It ought to be impossible to feel *this* in tune with him, to be sharing something so intimate with someone she barely knew. But this was something more than 'just sex'. More than a mere 'escape'. This was every bit as intense as she'd feared it would be. And it was fantastic.

'Please…' She arched her back. 'Oh, please.'

'So hot…' he muttered.

She arched again, so close. Hating and yet loving the chuckle that came from him. 'Jack…'

'I'll let you have it soon,' he promised. 'Soon…'

*'Now.'*

'Soon,' he growled.

But she knew she nearly had him now. His movements quickened, roughened, his skin was sweat-dampened. And the look in his eyes was all desperation.

'I want to feel you.' She squeezed him, locking him deep inside her, wrapping her arms more tightly about him so they were one.

He growled again, then thrust harder. Faster. Out of control and holding nothing back. He was lost to it now.

She threw her head back and let his passion overwhelm her. She heard his shout and victory shot through her. She closed her eyes and her body tightened on his for a split second longer before tumbling once more into that orgasmic abyss.

Long, long, long moments later she was still breathless,

still unable to move, despite the fact that he'd lifted himself away from her.

'Jack?' She reached a hand out to find him.

'I'm here.' He sounded close. And he sounded amused.

She opened her eyes and found him lying on his side, watching her, warmth in his eyes.

'Did I forget to mention I'm an insomniac?' he murmured.

She arched into his caress as he ran his hand down the length of her spine.

'You did.'

Somehow she found the energy to rise to her knees. Somehow she was filled with a freedom and a playfulness she hadn't ever felt.

'What a shame for you…'

She pushed him so he rolled onto his back and straddled him, leaning forward so she could whisper against his mouth.

'And a bonus for me…'

# CHAPTER SIX

JACK HADN'T BEEN kidding about the insomnia. Just after four in the morning he lay listening to her soft, regular breathing—as he had been for the last hour or so. They hadn't bothered to close the curtains and he could see millions of stars above the darkness that was the treetops.

Stephanie was curled against him, her back against his stomach. He rested his hand over her hip, happy to hold her close as she slept.

The selfish part of him wanted to wake her—the part that had pushed to keep her with him for the night. The urge to lose himself in her again bit deep. The pleasure he'd got from touching her, from pleasing her, had been so much more than he'd expected—and he'd expected a lot.

He'd got the oblivion he'd wanted. All thought had evaporated in the steam, together with the doubts, the demons, the endless wondering…the fear.

He loathed the vulnerability that sneaked up on him. It was why he kept busy—working, travelling, pushing a punishing pace so he'd fall into bed at the end of the day too tired to start thinking.

But in the quiet those thoughts came to torment him. And this week had been worse than ever. As he stood on the precipice of finally knowing—of finally meeting—the man he thought was his birth father he needed to escape to survive.

*She* was the only way he could get through this last most painful waiting.

But, much as he needed her this second, he couldn't

wake her. She'd been tired before they'd got here and, given how hard and far and fast he'd pushed her, he knew she needed rest. That last time he'd taken her they'd both fallen asleep within seconds of coming.

But he'd woken less than an hour later.

He tried to stay still, regulating his breathing to hers, enjoying the feel of her in his arms. Her softness warmed him. Her silken hair tickled his skin. He lost himself in sensual memory.

He hadn't been sure if she'd be brave enough to truly let go or if she'd be stifled by her need to look 'just so'. But she'd floored him. She had been so willing, ready—as if she'd been fantasising about fooling around with him for the whole day. Behind that polished façade was a woman with needs, and she'd succumbed to the heat between them with enthusiastic abandonment and sweetness…and with that bit of edge he'd sensed in their first meeting. And with *humour*.

Yeah, if he'd thought he was going to get a Steffi Leigh 'tick-the-list' screw he couldn't have been more wrong. It was as if she'd cast aside every care and just fallen into the sensations. He'd been helpless to do anything but follow her.

His erection ached. His skin felt stretched over all his body. But he forced himself to stay quiet—contrarily uncomfortable, yet satisfied—and waited for the birds to sing in the dawn. One form of torture replaced by another. Holding her, yet not doing what he ached to.

In the end he couldn't cope with her closeness any more. While it was still dark he stole out of the bed and pulled on his boxers, leaving her to sleep. He ordered breakfast and worked on his report, then quietly paced around the veranda and hoped she'd wake some time soon.

It was another two hours before she emerged. He looked up from his notepad and watched her walk towards him. How much he wanted her actually *hurt*.

She looked totally different from the perfectly coiffed,

selfie-ready socialite he'd met at the hotel yesterday. Same dress, sure, but now it was rumpled—less 'refined' looking. And she had more freckles on her nose, thanks to the lack of make-up. Her hair was loose and framed her face in a slightly wild cloud of strawberry blonde—glints of red caught the morning light and lit a fire within him.

And the sparkles in her eyes were all new. He took pleasure in knowing *he'd* been the one to put them there, together with that small, satisfied curve of her mouth.

But there was colour high in her cheeks. Surely she couldn't still be embarrassed?

He tossed his pad onto the table and stood to meet her. Stephanie Johnson was nothing like the Steffi Leigh persona she presented. She was much more expressive. Much more responsive, more serious, more giving.

And not nearly as worldly as she made out.

Maybe he shouldn't have pushed her to come with him here. Maybe he shouldn't have seduced her into staying. Maybe he shouldn't tease her now.

But he wanted to see that smile more.

'Morning.'

She couldn't quite look him in the eye. How was that possible after all they'd done through the night?

Instead she glanced at the laden tray on the table beside him and zeroed in on the pile of paperwork.

'This is what you're meant to be doing while staying here?' she asked, one eyebrow raised, a teasing lilt to her words.

'I do need to finish that report some time.' He sat back down in the chair.

'Some time?' She nodded. 'So my staying is saving you from your workaholic self?'

She was saving him from something far darker. But he didn't want to talk about it. This was purely for fun. So he teased, 'And the lack of WiFi here is going to save *you* from your internet addiction.'

She laughed at that, then sent him a shy yet coy look from under her lashes. 'How are we going to distract ourselves from withdrawal symptoms?'

'I can think of a couple of things we could do.'

He couldn't hold back a moment longer. He reached out and wrapped his hand round her slim wrist.

'Stay another night.'

He hadn't meant to just ask like that. Not so soon.

She didn't reply. But she didn't pull away either.

'There's nothing you have get back to in Melbourne, is there?' He waited. 'Your blog will last another day.'

She still didn't say anything.

'Stephanie?'

He pulled on her wrist and she stepped nearer.

Still not near enough.

'But you have all this work to do,' she said softly, her glance barely skittering over him.

There was always work to do. He always did more that he needed to.

'It was an excuse,' he admitted. 'I wanted to be alone. But then I decided I'd rather be with you.'

'I'm *so* gratified,' she said, with a touch of that edge.

He chuckled. 'Have something to eat?' He gestured to the fruit.

'In a minute.' She looked at him then—a slow, scorching look, from his face down to his bare chest, to the tightness of his once loose boxers.

And for the first time in his life he couldn't move. He didn't want her expression to change. He didn't want this moment to pass.

Only then it got better—because *she* moved, coming to sit astride his lap.

'At least stay the day...' He croaked out the words.

Want consumed him. His hands moved of their own accord, roving up her thighs, pushing the skirt up so he could feel her beautiful soft skin.

'Please don't torture me again.'

Her eyes looked large in her flushed face. She looked so thoroughly aroused his body winched unbearably tighter.

'Torture you?'

'Tease me until I say yes,' she clarified in a whisper.

'But there's such pleasure to be had in teasing you.' He shifted his thighs so he could get nearer to where he wanted. 'You're blushing again.' He laughed. Then sobered. 'You really *don't* do this often, do you?'

'If you mean act like a brazen hussy? Then, no.'

'What's with the puritanical streak? There's nothing wrong with two adults having some fun together.'

'I know.' She fell silent.

'You don't regret it?' His hands stilled as something cold settled in his stomach.

'Actually, I've discovered I *like* being a brazen hussy,' she whispered with a laugh.

And then she kissed him.

He groaned in relief. But as she kissed she rocked her sweet curves on him. Her cool hands skimmed down his heated chest. The timbre of his groan changed—to need. To desperation.

He clumsily pushed aside the straps of her crumpled dress. She lifted her arms to help him—until it was over her head, she was naked astride him and he could kiss her breasts.

Thank heaven she hadn't bothered with bra or briefs. Thank heaven he'd thought to put condoms on every available surface—including the table beside him.

But he couldn't get to them. She was too busy kissing him. And he was too busy enjoying the way she was writhing on him. He was going to come in another instant and he wasn't even naked.

'Who's doing the torturing now?' he asked roughly.

It was the glittering smile that did it—*so* Steffi Leigh.

He stood so quickly she yelped. He set her on her feet and spun her to face the forest. 'Hands on the railing,' he ordered gruffly.

She'd already put them there to balance herself. He scooped up a condom from under his papers and shoved his boxers down, was rolling it down him in a trice.

He didn't understand why his control was *lessening* the longer he was with her. Hadn't he had enough sex through the night?

Clearly not.

She turned her head and sent him a soft smile over her shoulder. He brushed her hair back, loving the way it hung down her pale back.

'I still want you so much,' he muttered, nudging her feet wider apart with his foot. 'Can't get enough of this.'

He tilted her hips and pushed inside her tight vice.

'Goooood…' She arched her back and chuckled.

Inexplicably, the sheer joy in her laughter made him want to punish her—to make her as breathless and needy as he was.

He thrust harder, faster, and her breathing changed. He played with her—ruthlessly tormenting her from behind—one hand on her breast, the other between her legs, until he could feel her whole body shaking in his arms, could feel her clenching tight on him. Until she screamed so loud a million birds took off from the trees, forming a glorious screen of colour.

The sound of beating wings surrounded them. But he was the one flying.

'I'll stay,' she whispered, resting her head on his shoulder when it ended. 'A few more hours.'

*Thank God.*

He wrapped his arms around her and pulled her back so she was fully leaning against him. Suddenly he was tired. He just wanted to fall back into bed. Maybe actually sleep for an hour or so.

'I need to let Tara know my plans,' she muttered, twisting free to step away.

He watched her as he walked with her back into the apartment. This was more than a responsible safety check-in with a friend. He saw anxiety in the backs of her eyes at those odd moments when she thought he wasn't looking. There was more going on. More that she didn't want him to know.

And he didn't want to know. Right?

But curiosity was normal. It was human nature to want to get to the bottom of a mystery.

He wanted to shrug it off. Wanted not to be drawn in. But she was holding something back from him.

It shouldn't matter. In a few hours she'd drive out of his life. They'd do any business negotiations over the phone or the internet and this would be over.

'It's too early to call anyone yet.' He ran his hand down her gorgeous back. 'I think we should have breakfast in bed.'

Stephanie hadn't wanted to waste another minute sleeping, but her body had given her no choice. Pressed deep into the mattress, so relaxed—so *sated*—it had been impossible to keep her eyes open.

Now she rolled, blinking, and realised the sun was streaming in through the wide windows. It must be mid-morning already.

And she was alone in the big bed again.

She hated that. She'd wanted to experience the pleasure

of waking in his arms. Of easing out of slumber with the delicious sensation of someone holding her. Someone caring.

*Stupid.*

This wasn't about caring. This was about sex. She just wasn't that experienced. That was the problem. She'd never been with a guy who understood a woman's body so well. A guy who revered her and took such pleasure in touching. Offering the gift of orgasm. Again and then again.

And again.

But she had to stay cool. There was no risk of her heart being involved. This was nothing but a pleasurable experience. One that she simply couldn't resist. She was, after all, only human. And after a taste of this kind of passion she wanted it once more. This fantasy...

She wanted more than the rest of the day. She wanted another night. Instead she reached for her phone. She'd better text Tara and let her know she'd be late. And she needed to text Dan.

Jack walked into the room. He looked sleepy-eyed but satisfied—one hot, dishevelled male. Now she understood what he'd meant when he'd said he wanted to see her messy and undone. She felt a primal pleasure in knowing she'd been the one to make him raw like this.

As his gaze swept the length of her his lazy smile turned piratical. Yeah, he'd enjoyed indulging in the bounty from his pursuit. She didn't mind, because she liked looking at him too.

He hadn't bothered shaving, nor had he bothered putting on a shirt, and she seriously wondered whether he'd bothered putting either boxers or briefs under those low-slung jeans... Wait a minute...

'Where did you get those jeans?' She sat up quickly, clutching her phone to her chest.

'I had my bag brought up overnight.'

Of course he had. Meanwhile *she* was going to be stuck

in a wrinkled dress and no knickers. It was a good thing the hotel staff were so discreet and there was no one to see her do the walk—or in this case the drive—of shame. She wasn't going home yet anyway.

'I had a couple items sent for you too.' He leaned against the doorjamb, a smile playing on his lips.

He'd *what*? 'When did you arrange that?'

'While you were sleeping.'

'Last night?'

Had she actually slept? It felt as if they'd kissed every minute of the night. Hours of touch and torment. Until she'd been unable to peel her body from the bed. Clearly *he* hadn't slept, though. He'd been plotting.

'What "items" did you have sent for me?' she asked, suddenly feeling chilled.

He sent her a sideways look, his grin flashing. 'Nothing major. Don't get too excited.'

Was he used to picking up women and whisking them away for the weekend? Buying them a few items of clothing to see them through? Did he then say goodbye with some horrendously expensive trinket for them to remember their trip fondly? Was *that* how he played this?

*Does it matter?*

All that mattered was enjoying the moment, right? Except it *did* matter…

'You don't have to wear any of it,' he said, coming forward and lifting her chin with his finger. 'Stay in your dress. Better still, stay in nothing. And stay another night.'

So full of tease. So tempting.

What would another night away hurt, when she'd had none since her brother's illness? She'd had not one night alone. Not one night out partying, or even going to the movies with a girlfriend. In the eighteen long months since their mum had left Stephanie had been there day and night in their tiny apartment, scraping together whatever work she could find online, so she was there to get his drinks of water, his food. To plump his pillows, put on a DVD… to talk to him.

But Dan hadn't got any better. His mood had plummeted. And she had no idea how to drag him from that pit of depression. Half the time he refused to take his medication. Refused to go to the meetings his physio had recommended. He was happy at home, he reckoned. But he wasn't. And neither was she.

'You okay?'

She glanced up and saw Jack frowning at the phone in her hand.

'Problems?'

'No, it's okay.'

She put all thoughts of her brother from her mind. Banished all thoughts of her blog, too. There was just this moment. And for once she was living in the moment—taking the advice she'd given online to others.

She'd be present—right here, right now.

She put the phone face-down on the table and slipped out of the bed, walked past him.

'I'm going to shower.' She glanced behind her and smiled at the arrested look on his face. 'I'd like company.'

His hands went to his jeans. 'Fantastic.'

Half an hour later she watched Jack bring a large glossy bag into the bedroom.

'Yours, if you fancy.' He half bowed and walked out.

Reluctant, yet curious, she lifted out the tissue-wrapped contents and placed them on the bed. There were a couple of dresses, still with tags on, one short, one long. Both slinky. Both designer. Both utterly gorgeous. Both eye-wateringly expensive. And both the right size.

Yeah, he'd *definitely* done this before.

Fighting the sinking feeling, she looked at the last item

in the bag. Navy silk pyjamas. Had he *really* thought she might want to wear something in bed?

Shaking her head, she contemplated the dresses for only a second before deciding.

He was leaning on the veranda, steaming coffee in hand, when she walked out to meet him.

'Not quite the perfectly tailored dress of yesterday, but comfortable, I hope?' He put his hands on her waist and pulled her flush against him.

'Very comfortable, thank you.' She glanced down at the silk pyjamas she'd put on. She'd knotted the bottom of the jacket to tighten it a little and slipped on her kitten heels. 'Any objection?'

She instantly regretted the question—why should she want to please him? Because he'd paid for them?

'None whatsoever.' He skimmed his palm down her back. 'They suit you.'

They covered her up more than either of the pretty dresses would have. And they were cool on her burning skin. Practical, right?

'There's more fuel in the car too,' he said idly. '"Under the Green Veranda anything is possible." Want to go on an adventure?'

'Yes, please,' she answered simply. She needed one last escape.

She followed him down the stairs and out into the bright sunshine to where the car waited.

'Any requests as to where we go?' he asked.

'Just drive. Anywhere but home.' And she didn't care how revealing that slip might be.

She no longer had to hide the way she liked to watch him drive. So she twisted in her seat so she could study his profile more easily.

He glanced at her and raised his brows. 'I *knew* you liked to look.'

Jack seemed pleased when she didn't deny it.

'So, travel guide guru, where are we going?' she asked.

'A real sanctuary,' he answered, his spirits lightening because she'd acquiesced so easily. 'An animal one.'

Emerald Springs was a tiny wildlife hospital only a few miles down the road from the Green Veranda. A private facility that specialised in the rehabilitation and release of injured wild animals.

Stephanie read the sign. 'It's closed to the public today.'

'We're not the public.'

He got out of the car and walked up to the main entrance.

'No?'

'We're patrons.'

She swivelled and looked at him with sharp eyes. 'You mean you gave them a heap of money so they'd let us come here today?'

'Pretty much,' he said blandly. 'Is that dreadful of me?'

He didn't wait for her answer. But he refused to think it was dreadful. It was for her pleasure.

'You must be Jack Wolfe.' A woman greeted them as soon as he walked in. 'We're so thrilled you could join us today.' She smiled at him broadly and lifted her hand to pat her hair. 'Just delighted.'

Jack smiled back at her.

It turned out she was the director of the facility, and she was happy to take them on a tour herself. She talked and talked as she showed them the surgery and the care suites.

'I cannot thank you enough,' she said to Jack, for the third time. 'Your contribution will make a huge difference to our work.'

He felt awkward, knowing Stephanie was eyeing him. 'It is, of course, an *anonymous* donation.'

'Of course.' The woman smiled and leaned a little too close. 'Just between us.'

Out of the corner of his eye he could see Stephanie's eyebrows arch, and she walked away towards a glass cage holding an enormous snake.

Jack extricated himself from the director with an apologetic smile and walked to stand next to Stephanie.

'They don't scare you?' he murmured.

'Of course they do,' she answered, not looking at him as she answered. 'But they're fascinating.'

He turned to look straight at her. 'Yes.'

'I think you wanted to see an echidna most especially?' The director interrupted the moment, her eyes only on Jack.

'Stephanie is very keen to see one, yes,' he said pointedly, watching the woman's smile dim a fraction.

Yeah, she seemed to have chosen to ignore the fact that he had a woman with him. And not just *any* woman.

He took hold of Stephanie's hand to emphasise it, pleased when he felt a teasing stroke of her fingers before she laced them between his.

'Of course.' The clinical director reverted to being a wholly professional tour guide with a smile. 'We have a very special treat for you today, Stephanie, if you want to put on a pair of those gloves…'

It turned out it was a baby echidna that had been rescued and was being hand-reared. It was so tiny it fitted into Stephanie's small hand.

Jack drank in her reaction, her glowing features. She was in raptures—definitely not too 'cool' to show enthusiasm. So refreshing.

'You *have* to hold this little honey,' she told him, all wide eyes and huge smile.

'I sure do.' He caught her eye briefly and then carefully took the tiny animal from her.

He knew she felt the sizzle—her flush gave her away.

'It's just *adorable*,' Stephanie said, staying near him to look down at the weirdest-looking little thing ever.

Jack knew they were timid creatures that curled up like hedgehogs when frightened. And, like hedgehogs, they had little spikes to warn off attackers. A very showy defence mechanism that kind of reminded him of someone else with painted armour.

Eventually the director spoke. 'I'm so sorry, but I'm going to need to get back to my office—and this wee one needs some rest.'

'Of course—thank you so much. We don't want to take up any more of your time,' Jack said smoothly.

'I'll get one of our volunteers to come down in case you have any more questions. You can stay as long as you like.' The woman smiled broadly at them both. 'And, Jack, thank you once again for your generosity.'

She put the echidna back into its cage and left.

Jack couldn't resist going up close to take another look at it.

'I thought you preferred to see creatures in their natural habitat?' Stephanie teased.

'She'll be back in the wild once she's big and healthy enough. Everyone needs help sometimes.'

'You know these babies are called puggles?' Stephanie brushed against him as she stood beside him. '*So* cute.'

'Uh-huh.'

He wasn't looking at the echidna. He was looking at the very sexy piece of femininity beside him. She was so hot and she had no clue. Or maybe she did. Because her green-blue eyes had turned smoky.

'You could at least *pretend* to be interested,' she said edgily.

'I'm fully interested,' he protested. 'Utterly enthralled. Every *inch* of my attention is snared—'

'You're *Steffi Leigh*!'

A high-pitched squeal interrupted them.

Jack turned and pulled on an automatic smile as a girl

walked across the room, looking as buzzed as if she'd had
a surprise party put on for her. Maybe in her late teens, she
wore a khaki tee shirt that had 'Emerald Springs Wildlife
Hospital Volunteer' emblazoned across it.

'Yes, I am.' Stephanie smiled at her. 'You read my blog?'

'Of *course* I do. We *all* do,' the girl practically sang.
'This is so cool—I can't believe you're here. Can I get a
picture with you?'

For a split second he wondered if Stephanie would say
no—given the whole lack of make-up thing. Not to mention the pyjamas.

'Absolutely.' Stephanie smiled at the girl. 'With the pug-
gle as well? Gotta go for the cute factor, right?'

She sent Jack a look.

'You want me to take the photo?' He stepped up and
took the phone from the girl.

'Yes, please,' Stephanie beamed, leaning in close to the
volunteer.

'Is he your boyfriend?' the girl whispered—too audi-
bly—to Stephanie as they posed together beside the echidna's cage.

'No, I don't have a boyfriend.' Stephanie maintained her
camera-ready smile, but the flush in her cheeks deepened.

'I'm working on it,' Jack drawled, sending them both a
wink from over the phone.

The girl's eyes widened and she giggled. Stephanie's
eyes shot daggers. She did not giggle. Jack had to bite his
tongue to stop himself laughing.

'You don't *want* to go out with him?' The volunteer
asked Stephanie, in another too loud whisper.

He tried to pretend he hadn't heard the disbelief in the
girl's tone.

'He's too good-looking and too successful,' Stephanie
answered blandly, avoiding Jack's eye and totally *not* whispering. 'Too used to getting everything he wants too easily.'

For a moment the girl's mouth hung open. Then she snapped it shut and cleared her throat. 'So… uh…is Tara here too?'

'Back in Melbourne.' Stephanie smiled at her and winked.

'Are you going to feature Emerald Springs on the blog?'

'I'm thinking I should—do you think so? Would it be helpful?'

She nodded. 'It would be *so* cool.'

'Then absolutely I will,' Steffi Leigh declared. 'I've got twelve fab things to list about the place already.'

'But it's okay for me to post this pic early?' the girl checked.

Jack was intrigued that she seemed so keen to please Steffi.

'Sure thing.'

He followed the two of them outside, listening to them chatter on and on about their favourite vlogs and number one lists. Eventually they hugged, and Jack took another photo of them by the car.

'Do you read her blog often?' he asked the young woman as he handed her phone back to her once she'd said good-bye to Steffi.

'*Always,*' she replied fervently. 'She's so funny. She's shorter than I realised. And quieter…'

'She's shy. More than you might think.'

And more reserved, yet at the same time *so* generous.

The girl's blush grew, but she nodded as if she'd known Steffi for years. Perhaps she sort of had.

'She's so, *so* lovely.' She suddenly switched to Steffi Leigh superfan and protector. 'She deserves the best.' She sent him a meaningful look.

'Absolutely.' Jack bit back a smile. He'd give Steffi Leigh his *very* best. Again and again and again. And soon.

The girl leaned forward and whispered conspiratorially, 'I think she likes you really.'

'I hope so,' he answered in a conspiratorial whisper back. And he realised he meant it.

He got into the car and glanced at Stephanie.

'Thanks for taking me there—it was lovely,' she said.

'My pleasure.' And it had been. He smiled as he turned out onto the road, enjoying the recollection of her chirping conversation. 'You get recognised often?'

'Fairly frequently—does that surprise you?'

It shouldn't. He'd seen the numbers on her followers. But her ease with it didn't seem to fit with that perfect, untouchable yet approachable image on screen.

'Does it stop you going to the mall?'

She chuckled. 'I don't tend to shop at the mall.'

'Where *do* you shop? One-off expensive boutiques?'

She frowned. 'No, op shops. Then I use my sewing machine. Half the time on the blog I'm in a black top, while Tara shows off some make-up tip. The rest of the time I'm showing off some second-hand restyled find. It's part of the fun.'

*Vintage, hip, cool. Quirky, personalised, stylish. Popular.*

All those words his marketing manager had thrown at him when presenting Steffi's blog as an option. All of them were accurate. Yet all of them were incomplete.

'You can't tell me the mint-green number is a second-hand store find?' It fitted her far too well.

'Well, no…' She laughed. 'That was made from an old pattern.'

'Made by you?'

She nodded.

More talents. He shouldn't be surprised, because today she was making a pair of pyjamas look couture just by the way she walked. The woman had innate style and the world stopped to look.

The world tuned in especially to look and listen.

And to laugh with her.

He'd thought Steffi Leigh was all superficial fluff and all fake, but Stephanie had been genuinely pleased to talk to that girl, and in doing so she'd made her day. She'd really cared about her—had been authentic. Genuine.

She *was* Steffi Leigh, and yet she was so much more.

'You're more of a mystery than I anticipated,' he murmured.

'No, I'm not.' She shot him an awkward look. 'What you see is what you get—Steffi Leigh.'

'But you don't look *all* Steffi Leigh today.' At her arched eyebrows he explained. 'No make-up.'

'You're not about to go on about how I don't need it, are you?' She eyed him warily. 'Because let me tell you make-up has its place and its purpose.'

'I think you look beautiful both with make-up and without.'

'Good answer.' She rewarded him with a softly blown sarcastic kiss.

She was the same—perky, upbeat, full of energy and enthusiasm. And so sexy that desire burned in his gut.

'Where are we going now?' She turned and stared straight ahead, in a very unsubtle attempt to change the topic.

'Food.' Though, starving as he was, his body was seeking another kind of sustenance.

*Down, boy.* He could go more than an hour without jumping her bones again, couldn't he? Maybe…?

Twenty minutes later he watched in silent amusement as she stared at the building and it's discreet signage.

'This is a *very* fine restaurant. French,' she noted.

'It is.'

'I cannot go in there in pyjamas.'

'Of course you can. You're Steffi Leigh—you can do anything.'

She turned and looked at him. 'Is that what you think?'

'Yeah. I do.'

He was rewarded with a smile in her eyes that was so heartfelt it made him melt. Hell, he was going soft. But when he saw emotion in her eyes like that he was spellbound.

'Welcome, Mr Wolfe.' The *maître d'* opened the door for them. 'We're thrilled to have you here today.'

Jack chuckled when he saw Stephanie almost grinding her teeth as the man ever so obsequiously led them to the private table he'd booked.

'You don't like it?' he asked her, as soon as the man was out of earshot.

'They all know who you are. They're all expecting you. They're all bowing and scraping and bending over backwards to do anything you want…' She trailed off as she looked across the table at him.

And suddenly she blushed furiously.

She was thinking about bending over backwards.

He laughed and reached out to take her hand.

'You make your money by selling tips to the independent traveller. The kind who is unafraid to doss down in a roach-infested hostel. But *you* only stay in hotels and luxury retreats. Five stars or more. And you dine at fine French restaurants.' She'd recovered enough to try to tease him. 'You're a fraud.'

'I thought I was keeping you in the manner to which you are accustomed?' He shrugged. 'Only the best for Steffi Leigh. The most refined… "Blogalicious" and all that.'

But he suspected she *wasn't* accustomed. And now his curiosity about her was like a white-hot iron brand, burning its mark deeper into his skin. Because the whole Steffi Leigh scenario didn't quite add up.

Her enthusiasm for everything was genuine, but it was almost a naïveté—as if she couldn't believe her luck at being here. Maybe he'd got a little jaded with all the travel, and hadn't seen it with fresh eyes in a while, but it was as if she'd been locked away and was breathing clear air for the first time in months.

And then there were those moments when she looked wary, catching her lip. As if she was afraid she was about to say something she shouldn't. He'd known that look all his life—when someone was keeping something back from him.

His parents had never, ever discussed his birth father. They'd told him they knew very little. That his birth mother had never wanted to talk about it. That they didn't even know his name.

But he knew that wasn't all they knew. They knew more—they just didn't want to tell him.

Stephanie didn't answer him now either, choosing to bury her nose in the menu instead. He gave her a few minutes and then asked which dishes she was mentally debating over.

'All of them…' she sighed.

'Really?' He waved and called the waitress over. 'We're going to do a banquet, if you don't mind. One of everything.'

'Jack—' Stephanie interrupted, sounding scandalised. 'We can't do that.'

'Sure you can.' The waitress smiled at Jack, her eyes glued to him. 'Sampler sizes of everything?'

'That would be perfect.' He smiled back and shot Stephanie a triumphant glance.

'She'd bend over backwards too…' Stephanie muttered beneath her breath as the woman walked away.

'You think?' He laughed. 'Too bad. I only want *you*. Backwards. Frontwards. Sideways. Any way. Every way.'

He looked at her and realised it was the truest thing.

He got as much pleasure out of watching her enjoy the meal as he did in tasting it himself. A few bites of each delicious dish. He laughed at her scolding him for such wastage.

'You're someone who can do anything,' she mused eventually, sitting back in her chair and gazing at a beautiful painting that hung on the wall near them. 'Is this what it's like for you all the time?'

'Hmm?'

'You just travel about, looking at the most amazing things, eating the most amazing things…having the best time ever.'

His heart warmed—she was having the best time ever. So was he.

'It's never like this,' he said honestly. 'Not usually as relaxed…it's busier. If I'm travelling it's usually to meet up with a few of the writers. There are meetings. I like to do some spot fact-checking… It's busy. I don't get to relax all that much. There's always something to think about. Some email to answer or a person to see.'

'But you're relaxed now?'

He nodded.

'So am I.' She smiled.

Something turned over in his chest. Suddenly he didn't want to think any more. Or talk. He needed to move.

'Let's go back to bed.'

She laughed and shook her head a little. 'So single-minded…'

Fixated? Yes.

'You've got to say it's a good idea.' He leaned forward.

'It's a good idea.' She nodded. 'A very good one.'

He was so glad she was on the same page.

*Sex.* That was all.

He summoned the waitress and asked for the bill. But the second the woman placed the slim leather folder onto the table Stephanie tried to snatch it up.

Jack stopped her by playing snap—smacking his hand down on hers. She might have got her hand on it first, but he was on top. And he wasn't giving it up. He felt her hand form a fist beneath his. And then she pulled her hand away.

'You've got to let me pay.' She looked ferocious.

'No, I don't,' he answered easily.

'Well, I'm not spending the day being treated like some…mistress or something.'

He was so surprised he laughed long and loud. Stephanie sat back, folded her arms across her chest and glared at him.

*'Mistress?'* he repeated with another chuckle. 'Like in some movie or something?'

She didn't like him paying. Was that why she'd picked the pyjamas over the designer dress?

Five minutes later he watched her stride ahead of him and get into the car. She slammed the door in a way the old car wouldn't appreciate. So *not* positive and enthusiastic Steffi Leigh now. She really was angry?

'I'll borrow the pyjamas for the day, and thank you for them, but that's *it*.' She sat with her arms folded and her nose in the air.

He liked the show of pride in what she would and wouldn't accept from him, but he wasn't above teasing her about it. 'Well, you could give them back to me *now* if they make you feel uncomfortable.'

She turned her head and met his challenge with fire in her eyes. 'Sure.'

# CHAPTER SEVEN

SHE STARTED TO unbutton the pyjama jacket. Jack stared at her, then quickly glanced around the car park. 'Someone will see!' He started to laugh.

'Then you'd better start the engine.' She tossed the silk pyjama top onto the back seat.

*His* engine was running red-hot already. And now she was wriggling out of the trousers…

'You'll burn your skin,' he said quickly. 'Your breasts.' All that creaminess. He couldn't bear to see it sun-damaged.

'I'm still wearing my bra.'

Yeah, but there was still too much skin—and she had *no panties* on. And he was finding it impossible to concentrate on the road.

She pushed her sunglasses up her nose and leaned back in the seat, a smile on her lips. But the heightened colour in her cheeks—that was embarrassment.

She was so damn independent—spirited, and determined to make a point. And she was so full of spontaneity.

He liked this side of her. A lot. And if that was the way she wanted to play it, who was he to argue?

Except he had to drive. He had to get them back to the hotel as fast as possible.

He glared at the road ahead. The sight in his peripheral vision was *killing* him. It wasn't just the nudity—the undeniable beauty of her—it was that *attitude*. That was what had him harder than rock.

'Put the jacket back on. You don't want to get sunburnt,' he all but pleaded five minutes later.

'Or get more freckles?' She nodded, but didn't reach for the jacket.

'You don't like them? That's why you cover them up with make-up?' He laughed. '*I* like them. I like going dot-to-dot with my tongue.'

Her lips parted as she drew in an audible breath. 'You make a case for letting them stay uncovered...'

He braked and pulled over to the side of the road.

'I won't forgive myself if you get sunburnt. The drive back is going to take too long...' And he wasn't going to make it. 'Stephanie...' He thought desperately. 'You know the sun is harsher here.' He looked down at her beautiful body. '*Please.*'

'Do you know about all the hazards in every country in the world?' she asked, relenting and pulling the pyjama top across her lap.

He sighed in relief and pulled back out onto the road again. 'I read through each book as it comes off the printer.'

'Every one? Every edition?'

'The buck stops with me. I'm known for my ability to spot typos that three proof-readers have missed.'

'They must love getting *those* emails from you.'

'Oh, I don't email.' He laughed at her dry tone. 'I call a face-to-face meeting and yell at them.'

She giggled. 'You *so* don't.'

'What do you *think* I do?'

'You flatten them with a look.'

'You think?'

'You can do the most withering arctic stare ever. I bet they dread it. You'd go all quiet and just look disappointed.'

He laughed, but oddly she was right. 'I have good staff— they don't like to screw up. They know they have the best

job in the world. Everyone who works for the company gets
to travel. It's part of the deal.'

'Even the proof-readers?'

'And the PAs. And the receptionist at head office…ev-
eryone.'

She looked amazed. 'And you too—all the time?'

'A lot—yeah. I have a desk in all our offices. I like to
keep moving. Keep them all on their toes.'

'Is there anywhere you haven't been?'

Was that envy in her voice?

'So many places,' he admitted. 'I try not to return to the
same place unless I absolutely have to. Obviously I have
meetings in the majors…but the only other place I regularly
return to—apart from home—is Indonesia.'

'To that orphanage?'

He nodded.

'Why that one?'

He hesitated as he turned into the track that would take
them to their hidden forest paradise. 'I was born in Indonesia. It's only by sheer luck that I wasn't one of those
kids. I had a mother who couldn't cope. A father who…'
He paused. 'Who was never in the picture. I was adopted
by the Wolfes. I was very lucky.'

He had been. He knew it. And he didn't want to hurt his
family by telling them of this search for his birth father.
But he needed answers. It was as if there was this one tiny
gap deep inside him and he didn't know how to fill it. Even
though he knew he had the love of his adoptive mother
and father and brothers, that he had friends, that he had an
amazing career…had it all.

Yet that gap remained.

And it was filled with fear. But knowledge—as always—was the key. He now had a report that didn't make
great bedtime reading. So he'd meet the man—find out the
truth for himself.

He could see her biting back her curiosity. Couldn't help answering the unspoken questions in her eyes even though it wasn't something he ever usually discussed.

'She was very young when she had me. She'd run away from home… She met my parents while she was travelling. They travelled together and they helped her straighten out for the pregnancy. At the time Irene and Ed—my parents—didn't think they could have children. My birth mother—Lisa—tried initially to keep me, but she couldn't give me what she knew they could. So she gave me to them.'

He tightened his grip on the steering wheel.

'She visited often…but in the end she couldn't control the demons hounding her…' He shrugged. Eventually she'd relapsed and unintentionally overdosed. 'I was very lucky to have two mothers who loved me. That's more than many people get.'

Stephanie was silent. But it was an easy silence, not awkward. And somehow he ended up telling her more.

'And, as sometimes happens, only a few months after adopting me my adoptive mom got pregnant. Twins. My brothers are amazing. James does urban search and rescue. He's a total hero. And George…he's crazy. He invests in things. He's a lot of fun.'

'They didn't want to work in the company?'

He shook his head. 'Both wanted to do their own thing. Mum and Dad supported them in that.'

'But you wanted to go into the family business?'

'I guess I got the travel gene from my birth mother. Working for Wolfe Guides ensures plenty of travel.'

He pulled up in front of the apartment, feeling more exposed than her—which was crazy, given she was only a scrap of fabric away from total nudity.

Finally he gave himself permission to turn and look at her square-on.

She was watching him, her eyes big and soft and caring, and so much more than Steffi Leigh he almost couldn't bear to look into them.

'Do you feel like you owe them?' Stephanie waited half a beat before apologising. 'Sorry, that was a stupid question.'

How could she possibly think she could understand *any* of the complex relationships this man had?

'No. It's okay. I do. Sure I do. But they don't *expect* me to work for them or anything.' He smiled.

Maybe some of the reason why he worked so hard was out of a sense of duty. She could respect that. She could understand that.

'No—'

'It's okay—I know you didn't mean it that way.' He leaned towards her. 'You thinking of putting clothes on any time soon?'

Laughing, she shook her head.

It didn't help her like him less. She was *so* crushing on him now. Like every other woman they'd seen today. They'd all taken one look and fallen under his spell.

As for that image of him standing cuddling that tiny echidna so carefully...? It was seared on her eyeballs. At the time her ovaries had all but exploded. His affinity with and protectiveness for the vulnerable spoke volumes about him.

And it contrasted with the all-business, tolerate-no-frippery stern man who'd introduced himself in the hotel foyer. Ruthless, bossy—sure. And he was totally used to getting his own way. To being the most powerful person in the room.

But he could be tender too.

Shame that the guy lived on the other side of the world. That he wasn't interested in anything more than a fling.

She'd seen all those people today, running to do as he'd bid. The thing was, even if he hadn't been wealthy they'd have still done anything and everything for him. He just had that presence. Charisma. So striking.

And, yes, the undeniable aura of power.

And the life he led… Donating to charity here and there, dining at fine restaurants every night, staying in exclusive invitation-only resorts…

He was in the top one per cent of the world. Utterly elite in every way. And so totally out of her league.

Good thing she was going home tomorrow. Back to reality. Back to Dan.

'I have a brother,' she said softly, thinking aloud as she shrugged her arms back through the pyjama jacket and got out of the car.

'Yeah? What's he like?' Jack asked, walking round to meet her.

Stephanie hesitated, swaying towards telling him the truth. That her brother was broken and she didn't know how she could make him whole again. That yet again she wasn't able to be all that a person needed.

But Jack clearly had a couple of issues of his own and he'd worked through them. He was determined to be master of his own destiny. That kind of coping was something she ought to emulate. He didn't need a self-indulgent sob-story from her. So she thought back to what Dan had been like—before the illness.

'He's an amazing athlete. Really fast and strong.' She smiled as she remembered the good days. 'Seriously, there's no sport he doesn't excel at. When we were younger we spent every weekend at some swim meet or other, then basketball in the evening, athletics, cricket… He was the sun. Our calendars revolved around his events.'

He'd been so active. And the apple of their parents' eyes. But after their father died her mum had immediately got into a relationship with one of Dan's coaches and their lives had become even more sport-crazy.

'Did you play too?' Jack took her hand and walked her around the side of the apartment to the private turquoise pool, with the lush forest as its backdrop.

'Oh, no.' She laughed. 'I wasn't blessed with that same athletic physique or aptitude. He's gifted, you know?'

And he'd worked so hard. It had been his everything.

'So what did you do while he was playing?'

'I tagged along and sat on the sidelines and started my lists. "The Five Best Cafés near the Melbourne Cricket Ground" or something. It was fun.'

She'd enjoyed taking her camera and seeing parts of the country she wouldn't normally have got to. And she'd taken her bag of design books and her crafty things and got on with it.

'So, has he been snapped up by a team? Or gone to university on a sports scholarship or something?'

She forced herself to nod, unable to speak. Because Dan had lost all those chances.

She turned and dived into the pool, escaping answering properly.

When she surfaced he was standing by the edge of the water and watching her with a frown in his eyes.

'Your parents must be proud of you too,' he said.

She laughed, unable to hide the bitter edge. 'Why?'

'Your blog.'

She turned to float on her back. 'Mum doesn't really get it. She's on her third marriage. She lives in France. She always needs a husband. She doesn't like to be alone.'

She'd wanted a partner—not children. She hadn't been able to cope with Dan once he'd lost his limbs. Hadn't been able to cope with the moods and the depression. She'd found another man to whisk her away...put him before anyone else.

'What about your dad?'

'He passed away a few years ago,' she said. 'Cancer. It was very quick.'

'So just you and your brother live in Australia now?'

'Yeah.'

'And you blog full-time?'

'I dropped out of university when the blog really took off,' she said.

But it hadn't been the blog. It had been after Dan's illness.

'What were you studying?'

'Art history, design—some straight history papers as well.'

'What were you wanting to do with it?'

'Teach, I guess…' She shrugged. 'Or work in a gallery or something.'

'But now you teach on your blog?' he teased.

'Hardly.' She rolled her eyes. 'I just write lists.'

'You want to travel,' he said.

He'd seen that? She shrugged, as if it wasn't really what she'd always wanted to do.

'You want to go and see paintings…you want to go to Florence and Paris and New York.'

'Who *doesn't* want to go to Florence and Paris and New York?' She laughed, slipping back into Steffi Leigh. 'Think of the shops, the fashion—'

'And the art, the history.' He waggled a finger at her. 'You're not as shopping-shopping-shopping as you pretend.'

'I don't pretend.'

'No,' he said thoughtfully. 'But you don't present all parts of yourself. Not on the blog.'

Of course she didn't. 'Some things should always remain private.'

'A passion for art doesn't need to remain private.' He pulled off his tee and tossed it down by the corner of the four-poster daybed. 'You filter everything you put online.'

'Doesn't everyone?'

'Perhaps.' He slowly unbuckled his belt. 'You should trust yourself—you have more to offer than just lists.' He shoved his jeans down and kicked them off. 'You don't want to go back and finish your degree?'

*More than anything.* But even more than that she wanted Dan to take up some kind of study—for him to envisage some kind of future beyond just sitting on the sofa. Her brother still had so much to offer the world…he just had to imagine it.

'Maybe later,' she breezed, brushing off the query. 'I don't have time right now.'

'And no boyfriend?'

'Not in real life,' she tried to joke.

'No time for that either?'

*Exactly.* But, in truth, Dan wasn't the only reason why she kept her heart free. 'You don't want to inherit your birth mother's addiction—I don't want to inherit *my* mother's problems either,' she said.

'What's her problem?'

'She's dependent on men.' She cleared her throat. 'She couldn't bear to be alone after my father died. She remarried a few months later. When that didn't work out she remarried again. Within a few months.'

*And didn't give a damn about what her kids thought of it.*

Dan had buried himself in his sport—pushing himself further and faster until his whole identity had been bound up in being a great athlete. So when the illness had robbed him of that he'd felt he was nothing. Had nothing to offer.

Stephanie had buried herself in her blog—hiding out in her room and dreaming up all kinds of daft lists…entertaining herself, her friends, and eventually a whole bunch of strangers. But she'd decided not to be her mother *ever*—not to have that inability to stand on her own, to be that infatuated.

Never happening.

'She chose a man over her kids,' she said crisply. 'Any man rather than be alone.'

Sure, it hadn't been as if they were little kids. Both had finished school. But then her brother had become an invalid.

'So you've opted for the "nothing" rather than the "all"?' Jack asked.

'I'm very busy with my blog.'

'But you have needs, Steffi Leigh.'

He dived in and swam underwater to surface right beside her.

'You've not seen my list for "A Single Girl's Satisfaction".'

'What does it say?'

'It gives the five best "personal products" for the single woman.'

He laughed. 'I'd better go read that blog when we get back to the city.'

'I'm sure you'll find it informative.' She smiled.

He pulled her towards him, holding her so she couldn't float away. 'You must have had a boyfriend in the past, though. Right?'

His eyes were very navy now. So watchful.

'At university, sure.' But there'd been only the one.

'What was he like?'

She'd been a late bloomer—she'd been at an all-girls school, giggling her way through the years with Tara at her side. Tara had been the one who'd attracted the guys in those years. Stephanie's mum had been the one out dating.

'He wanted more than I was willing to give.'

She'd finally agreed to go out with a guy in her history class. He'd been asking her for ages and he was a nice guy. She'd thought she could handle it—not fall too deep. And she hadn't.

She was not going to be the kind of woman who abandoned her children, her career, her country to follow her latest great passion. She'd stay and see to her responsibilities.

In the end her boyfriend had said she was too distant. That she didn't give him what he needed. That she always put him last.

She probably had.

'What didn't you want to give?' Jack asked.

She shook her head.

After it had ended she'd focused on building her blog. Taking photos for it, dreaming up ridiculous list topics and then talking them up in the vlogs. And now, after Dan's illness, there was no time, no occasion to meet men.

'What about you? Millions of girlfriends, I bet.' She batted her lashes at him, hoping he'd drop the subject.

'Holiday flings,' he corrected. 'Never anything long-term or serious. Work always comes first for me.'

'Ditto.' She blinked at him again, so very Steffi Leigh.

He chuckled.

She was tempted to tell him all about Dan. But her mother was so needy. Her brother was so needy. She didn't want to be like that. Didn't want to dump on him. Besides, despite how strong he appeared, he had his own anxiety—she'd seen it before that first meeting.

That stark loneliness?

It had almost hurt her with its intensity. She wasn't adding to his burden.

She wasn't doing to him—or to anyone—what her brother had done to her. And her mother.

'Come on, you've had way too long in the sun. There's a bed just here. Let's make love al fresco again.'

'We're not making love—we're having sex.' And she was reminding *herself* of that more than anything.

He frowned. 'We're making *nice*.'

She chuckled. 'Okay, we're making good.'

'*So* good.'

She wound her arms around him, pulling him close to kiss him so she couldn't spill her secrets.

She wanted to tell him everything. She wanted to trust him. To lean on him.

And she couldn't.

# CHAPTER EIGHT

'THIS PLACE IS so beautiful it doesn't feel real.'

Jack stirred and sat up to look at her. *She* was so beautiful it didn't feel real. Tousled and smiling up at him, tangled in a white sheet, she was an irresistible treat he couldn't taste enough.

They were resting on the daybed, the forest and pool largely hidden from view by the white drapes. It was as if they were living in a cloud. Heaven.

'It's like something in a movie,' she added in a soft murmur. 'Everything is so perfect.'

Not quite everything. She was leaving soon and he'd be alone this last night.

'You watch a lot of movies?' he asked, clutching at this conversational straw to keep the dread at bay.

A faraway look entered her eyes. 'I see a few...'

He wanted her to keep talking—anything light and airy that would keep him distracted. 'I love movies.'

'They're your "jam"?' She rolled over and teased him. 'You don't strike me as a movie person.'

'Why not?' he asked. 'I travel on planes a lot—what else is there to do?'

'Don't you spend every hour in the air working?'

'A few hours, sure. But there are some long flights. Work hard, play hard. Movies are play, right?'

'*Women* are play for you.' She stretched her arms out wide on the mattress. 'A couple of days like this—your holiday flings. I bet you have them all the time.'

'Not at all.'

She threw him a laughing look.

Indignation rose. He'd never done this—never with a potential business associate. And he'd never had as much fun either.

'Come here.' He pulled her flush against him and rolled, trapping her beneath him.

Satisfaction thrummed. This was where he wanted her. Her length to his, with those gorgeous lips within easy kissable distance.

He made the most of it. Again.

'What *is* your jam, then, if not movies?' he asked, still needing to keep it light, keep it easy.

'Art and design books. I shop online for them. They're my guilty pleasure.'

She was *his* guilty pleasure. 'Online? You don't browse for hours in some fancy bookshop and decide which ones you want over some complicated coffee order?'

Something shadowed her eyes, but she forced a laugh. 'I don't have time.'

Because she was such a busy blogger, always out and about, compiling pictures and data for her lists?

He tried to smile but the dread was setting in. He didn't want her to leave. He'd spent almost all day not thinking about his meeting tomorrow, thanks to her.

And right now he didn't care that his muscles ached from the acrobatics of last night. He just wanted to stay locked away with her like this.

His sex drive had roared to life from the moment he'd first laid eyes on her, and now the need was spiking higher the nearer the end loomed.

'Stay another night,' he whispered, unable to hide that edge of desperation.

He hated the way she dropped her gaze, shutting him out. He felt tension stiffen her body, and she pushed at his shoulder so he'd shift off her.

'Don't worry about the blog.' He felt certain that whatever it was she *wasn't* saying was related to that.

She nibbled her thumbnail and gazed through a gap in the drapes, obviously thinking. Obviously deciding.

All Jack could do was hold his breath. He wasn't going to 'torture' her into saying yes again. He wanted her to *want* to stay—and to be able to say it.

'If I sell "The List" to you, there's nothing more for us,' she said suddenly—super-decisive. Super-businesslike. 'And I'll walk away from the blog entirely.'

His blood chilled. Nothing more for them? Okay. He could take that rejection like a man. There wasn't supposed to be anything more for them beyond this anyway.

But he'd seen for himself how much she enjoyed interaction with her readers, how dedicated she was to her blog. Was she worried that things might be awkward because of their affair?

He wasn't letting that happen. She wasn't walking away from something she loved and had worked hard for because of this couple of days.

They meant nothing, right?

'You don't have to walk away from it. If you're worried about this affecting your work in the future, then don't. I live in the States. I spend a lot of time travelling. More than likely we won't see each other again.'

He felt his stomach drop as he said it. But it was the truth and it was a good thing. This was only a fling. A distraction.

He'd expected her to withdraw more from him because he'd spoken so bluntly, but now she rolled to face him.

Even though she'd stopped biting her nail, she looked even more worried. 'There's something you should know.'

His heart thudded, striking an uncomfortably fast beat. She wanted to tell him something important. And he wanted to hear it too much.

From the look on her face it wasn't something awesome.

'I get a lot of help with the blog.' She reached down and pulled the loose top sheet up around her.

He waited.

'From my friends. I can't get to all those places myself. They call it in for me. Email me recommendations. I always verify…always take the time to get a second opinion…but the truth is the lists aren't all my own work. Not any more. And Tara with her make-up tips—that's such a big part of it now…' She drew in a sharp breath. 'So, you see, I'm a fraud.'

*This* was what she'd been holding back from him? That was *it*? He tried to hide his smile. 'You're not a fraud.'

She had more integrity than most people—her 'confession' told him that.

'I am,' she argued. '"Steffi Leigh" doesn't do everything on her blog. Not at all.'

'*Everybody* has assistants. Even the most creative people get their ideas from seeing places, meeting people. I'd be more concerned if you *didn't* outsource some of the work.' He was amazed she'd thought this was a problem. 'Steffi Leigh' was more sweet than sharp. He brushed back her hair. 'There's nothing wrong with having help to get everything done.'

'There is if you take advantage of the people helping.' The shadows in her eyes deepened. 'If you take too much.'

'I don't think a few café recommendations is asking too much from your friends,' he teased. 'Blogs are notoriously difficult to maintain over time. Even I know that.'

She gazed up at him and smiled slowly. 'Even you, huh?'

'Stay the night. I have to be back in Melbourne tomorrow, so I can drive us in the morning.' He wanted her to stay with him right up 'til the meeting. He needed her to. He needed the distraction or he was going to go insane.

Her smile faded. 'Jack, I need to—'

'Check in with Tara—I know.' He cut her off before she could frame any reason to reject his request. 'But *stay*.'

She was silent for so long, and it was killing him not to kiss her again. To tease her. But he couldn't do that this time.

He used every ounce of his willpower to stay still when she reached out and placed her hand on his cheek in the gentlest caress.

'I can't say no to this,' she whispered, her eyes so deep in colour. So tortured.

'To this?' he leaned closer.

'To you…' she breathed.

*Thank goodness for that.* With a groan he kissed her. He felt her immediate response. And he sank into it.

He wasn't beside her. *Again.*

For a moment Stephanie lay there and let disappointment hit. Stupid to miss something she'd never known. But just once she'd wanted to wake with him beside her. And this was their last ever night.

She checked her phone—to find out the time and to make sure there was no further message from Tara.

It was just after two-thirty in the morning. Time to be sleeping—not up working or worrying. She suspected she knew which of the two he was doing.

They'd had a gorgeous evening. Another decadent meal had materialised while they'd bathed together in that magnificent bathtub. They'd eaten, laughed. Talked about all things random and ridiculous. He'd seemed to be determined that they have a good time. And they had.

But all the while the ache in her heart had been deepening and her conscience tightening.

She'd been going to tell him about Dan this afternoon on the daybed. Just after she'd told him about her help with the blog she'd been going to admit it all.

But he'd interrupted her. And then he'd looked so boyishly happy when she'd agreed to stay another night it had taken her by surprise. And flooded her with pleasure.

She hadn't been able to bear to bring them both down.

Now she put the phone back on the small table beside the bed. It was almost out of battery and she didn't have a charger. No doubt those discreet, supply-everything-you-could-ever-want hotel assistants could fetch one, but it wasn't long until she'd be home again and this would be over and become nothing but memory.

A dream couple of days.

She wrapped herself in a sheet and tiptoed out through the open doorway.

He was leaning back in one of the wicker chairs. There was a pile of papers on the table beside him, but given he hadn't turned on a lamp she figured he wasn't bothering with work. He looked lost in thought.

Unhappy thought.

But he looked up when she paused a few paces away.

'You can't sleep?' she asked.

'Insomniac,' he half joked. But he sounded flat.

'You're worried?'

'You're astute.'

'Not really. People who wake in the small hours are usually worried about something.'

'So what are *you* worried about?' he asked.

'Getting cold,' she smiled weakly.

But waking without him again had already made her cold. And looking at him now smote her heart. She wanted to wipe away the tortured expression that he was no longer able to mask.

She knew that intense loneliness and despair. She wanted to see him smiling, relaxed, laughing, sated. However she could.

The one way she was *certain* she could.

'So many stars overhead,' she murmured.

'You revel in all of it, don't you?' he muttered. 'All that enthusiasm…it's real…'

'That's because it's beautiful,' she said simply.

'So are you.'

She shook her head.

'You *are*.' His voice sounded rough. 'Right now you're like a pearl, gleaming in the moonlight.'

'It's the pale skin,' she joked. 'Glows in the dark.'

'The dress, the make-up, the finish suits you…but so does this…' He stretched out his arm and grabbed her hand, drawing her closer. When she was near enough he slid his fingers through her hair. 'So beautiful.'

'You're half blinded by the darkness.'

'Just take the compliment,' he growled. 'Or do you want more?'

'You know what I want more of,' she murmured, her voice suddenly husky.

*She* knew exactly what she wanted. And she was doing it. She moved to stand between his feet, then knelt, letting the sheet drop in a pool around her as she did so.

She heard his indrawn breath.

'Stephanie—'

'Just let me,' she interrupted, and ran her hands up his shins and over his knees. 'You've done it for me so many times already.'

'Not that many. Not enough.' He put his hands on her waist. 'And I like it.'

She pushed his hands away, knowing he wanted to lift her to his lap, but she wasn't having it this time. She pressed her hands on his hard abs and pushed. 'I like it too. So let me.'

He sank back into the chair.

Pleased, she smiled. Now she could explore him before being submerged in her own sensations. Now she could have the pleasure of taking him to those dizzying heights first for once. She'd relish the chance.

She stroked up his long, muscled legs. He had such a strong, fit body. 'What do you do to work out?'

'Run, mostly,' he answered huskily. 'You can run anywhere.'

'And see the sights while you do it?'

He nodded, his head falling back on the chair as she kissed him, moving her mouth nearer and nearer his rigid length.

'You like being naked outside,' she teased, so pleased to find him hot and hard and straining for her touch.

'So do you.'

She chuckled, because he was right. He'd unleashed her inner nudist. Her inner sensualist. And now she utilised all her senses—to touch, taste, and to talk to him. Muttering her appreciation of him, telling him what she wanted to do to him.

Maybe it was moonlight madness, but she felt so free—to tease…to take. She listened to his increasingly ragged responses—his quickened breathing—savoured the scent of his arousal. His every reaction—physical, verbal—sharpened her own.

His hands toyed with her hair and she tilted her head to let him run his fingers the length of it. That he so obviously liked it thrilled her.

Because she liked *him*. She liked making him tense up, making him groan, making him mutter his need. His pleasure.

'Stephanie…' It was a warning.

But she didn't stop. She was never stopping. Not until she'd tasted all he had to offer.

'Stephanie!' He thrust, then arched, locked in a rigid, agonised battle. 'I can't—'

His hands tightened, twisting painfully in her hair.

But she didn't stop. And he didn't pull her away. She held him, one hand spread wide on his chest, seeking to touch as much of him as she could, her other hand rubbing, holding him still enough so she could suck him, take him as deep into her mouth as she could.

Until he groaned harshly.

And capitulated to the ferocity of her caress with a force all his own.

Then there was only the sound of his deep ragged breathing.

Slowly she knelt back and lifted her face to see into his.

'I lose myself in you,' he said raspily, with utter relief evident in his lax body.

'And that's a good thing?'

'Yes.'

'What is it you're escaping from?' she asked.

She was a temporary release—she got that. And that was good, because anything longer and she'd fall too hard.

'Fear.'

Swiftly he reached down and used his impressive strength to lift her into his arms. He sat her sideways across his lap.

'Being alone tonight,' he added, wrapping his arms around her and drawing her close against his chest.

She rested her head on his shoulder. 'I thought you valued your independence?' He was Mr Holiday Fling after all.

'Mostly I do. But tonight…'

'Why tonight?'

She lifted her head to see into his eyes, but he'd turned his face away. She cupped his roughened jaw and turned his face back towards hers. His skin was dampened with sweat—but she wasn't sure if that was because of her, or because of whatever nightmare it was he was locked into.

'Jack?'

'I'm meeting my birth father for the first time tomorrow.'

He expelled a harsh breath. 'He doesn't know I'm coming. He thinks it's a business meeting. Mum and Dad don't know that's why I've come to Australia. No one knows.'

Shocked, she tried to keep her own breathing even. 'Why don't they know?'

'I'm not sure if he knows I ever existed, and from what I've read he might not be that interested.'

Her heart broke for him. No wonder he was so edgy. 'What makes you say that?'

'All reports suggest he's ruthless.'

'Not everyone is as their PR might make them seem… we both know that.'

'I know. But there are…' He hesitated. 'Other things.'

She waited, watching. Willing him to keep talking—because she suspected he needed to. And she wanted to listen.

'My adoptive parents always denied they knew anything about him. Not even his name,' he said in a low voice. 'Whenever I asked they denied it. Then they changed the subject.'

'You think they lied to you?'

'Not lied. Just…didn't tell me. Not even their suspicions. After a while I stopped asking and decided to find out for myself.' His breathing picked up again. 'I hate it that they held it back from me. I know they probably thought they were protecting me, but not knowing is worse. I need to know.'

And right now he didn't. But it was clear he had some pretty scary suspicions.

'You're worried you'll upset them?' she asked. 'Is that why you've not told them?'

He nodded.

Her heart broke again. 'So… Tomorrow?'

'Yeah,' he half grunted.

'No wonder you can't sleep.' Who could sleep the night before something so momentous? No one human could.

'Is this related to that phone call you took when we first met in the hotel?'

He nodded.

No wonder he'd sounded so gruff. No wonder he'd wanted frivolous, frisky company these last couple of days. Who wouldn't?

And no wonder he'd been so restless the whole time they'd been together.

She looked into his eyes. Even in the weak starlight she could see that stark expression had returned.

*Need.*

One need she *could* fulfil for him. Physical. And just for tonight emotional.

She could care for him so easily. She liked him. It would be the tiniest step to open up to a deeper emotion. And she took it, not caring about any future cost to herself. His need for connection was greater than her need for protection.

'Let me distract you,' she said. 'I can help you escape…'

Together they could escape everything for just a few more hours.

She knew he wanted it—could feel him hard again beneath her butt.

'Are you sure?' he asked.

She half laughed as she slipped off his lap and turned to face him. Bending down, she kissed him, then drew back. In the starlight she sought out another condom from the stash that had been on the table that morning. She handed it to him. 'Let's pretend there's only tonight. Only now.'

But it was no pretence, really. Because for them that was all there would ever be.

When he was ready she straddled him, her knees either side of his hips, keeping herself balanced by holding on to his broad shoulders. The position rendered her so exposed to him. His hand on her spine pushed her forward, sealing her chest to his. He threaded his fingers through her hair, holding her head so he could see her.

Silence fell between them. There was only touch and taste and sight—and something so much bigger it had to remain unspoken.

She didn't kiss him. Didn't initiate any foreplay. There was only one thing that was right in this moment.

Slowly, holding that intense eye contact, she slid down on him, joining with him, taking him deep inside her— heartache, worry, everything.

She quivered. Her breathing quickened and she felt him tense in response. She tried to relax, but the feeling of him full and deep inside her overwhelmed her.

So intense. So big. So good.

He didn't buck upwards. She didn't ride. There was just a long appreciation of that sublime sensation of being locked together so tightly nothing could come between them.

Nothing but peace. Nothing but profound joy.

She looked into his eyes for a long, quiet moment of communication—unable to break away, unable to move. Utterly lost in the bliss of the moment.

Slowly his hands swept up her sides to cup her breasts. His thumbs teased in decadent slow circles around her tight nipples until eventually she had to move. Her dance began slowly enough, but his fingers forced the tempo until she had to writhe above him, her desperation to feel the plea- sure of his hardness beneath her, within her, increasing insanely quickly.

Always with him she was so quick.

She gasped as he worked a hand between them to help her. Only a few strokes had her hurtling too quickly to- wards orgasm.

'Not yet…' she breathed, breaking the wordless joy. 'Please.'

'You're not ready?'

'I want to enjoy this longer… You feel so good. You make *me* feel so good.'

She saw the flash of his smile in the starlight.

'Anything,' he muttered, a rusted steel thread in the darkness. 'I'll do anything you want.'

'Feel me,' she whispered.

She wanted to touch, to be touched. She wanted not to be alone. She wanted to *be* with him. And she wanted it to *last*.

'I do. I am,' he promised.

He kissed her, used his teeth to tease her lower lip so she opened for him.

She couldn't *not* open for him. She immersed herself in his kisses. And she tried to give—letting the desire she felt for him flow, releasing it all in the way she kissed and touched and clutched. She couldn't get near enough, couldn't adore him enough. She kissed and kissed and kissed him—with her mouth, with her body, she took him deeper every way she could.

He suddenly tightened his hold on her and stood up. He took the few paces inside to lay her on the bed, falling with her so their connection wasn't lost.

'Nothing has ever felt as good as this,' he muttered against her mouth.

'Then why have you stopped?' she asked.

'Sweetheart, I haven't even started…'

Jack let his fingers trail the length of her spine, gently stroking down, then up, then down again. He loved the feel of her warm, smooth skin. He loved her generosity, her untrammelled passion. He'd given her what she'd wanted—he'd touched her, felt her, drawn out the pleasure for them both, holding off that inevitable conclusion until she'd been almost in tears and begging. He'd never been so determined to satisfy someone—to *be* with someone in that way. So open. And then they'd come together.

Bonded together.

Tomorrow he would be meeting the man who was his birth father. Finding out answers he was terrified of. But maybe meeting him wouldn't be so bad. Maybe with a fairy princess at his side anything might be possible.

In her arms, in this moment, he realised he actually didn't care any more. That aching hole inside him—the one usually filled with fears, doubts and distressing imaginings—was gone.

All that mattered was being here with her. Seeing her smile and knowing she felt as close to him as he did to her. Feeling her relax against his body, blanketing him with her softness. Her fresh scent. With her silken flame-threaded hair trailing across his chest.

She'd fallen asleep. He hadn't. But now it didn't bother him and he refused to rouse her again. His body was replete, his soul soothed, just by holding her.

She'd given him something no one else ever had. He'd never felt as close to another person as he had in those moments with her. As if she understood the worry, the fear. She'd absorbed them and somehow they'd disappeared.

None of it mattered any more. Not now. He felt peace.

His eyelids lowered as finally sleep caught him in its clutches. On the very brink, he tightened his arms instinctively, holding her close.

And, like a talisman, she kept the nightmares at bay.

# CHAPTER NINE

'JACK.' STEPHANIE LEANED over him. 'Jack, I think we need to get up.'

The sun was streaming through the window and, as reluctant as she was to wake him, she knew there was no way he'd want to miss his meeting.

His eyes flashed open and an expression of shock shot into the vivid blue depths.

'Hell, I fell asleep.' He rubbed a hand over his face. 'I *really* fell asleep.

She nodded and sat up, reluctantly taking her hand off his chest. 'We need to get going if we're going to get back to town in time...'

'Yeah.' He frowned and pulled himself up into a sitting position beside her. He rubbed his face again. 'Thanks.'

Stephanie slipped from the bed. 'I'll just take a shower.'

'Sure.' He didn't demur, didn't try to pull her back into an embrace, didn't try to follow her.

From the distracted look on his face she knew he'd mentally checked out of their fling already. It was all over. Time to get home and get on with it.

But her heart was struggling to catch up with that concept. It ached to be back in bed with Jack.

For so many reasons that couldn't happen.

She stood under a cold shower and tried to snap herself out of it. It was just sex. Nothing more. Last night had been a one-off. He'd needed contact. She'd given him everything she had.

But she realised now that honesty was super-important

to him. And she hadn't been honest. It wasn't that she'd lied. She just hadn't told him everything.

Just as his parents hadn't for all those years.

But Stephanie's omission didn't matter, right? Dan wasn't relevant to the blog deal—to what Jack needed to know about her in the next few hours. And it was nothing on the intensely personal information he was seeking now. Not for him at least.

It didn't matter.

She had to remember that any connection she felt for him was just temporary. Just physical. An interlude.

She dressed quickly so he could have the bathroom.

Ten minutes later she looked up from her contemplation of the trees as he walked out to the deck. He was back in his suit. Like her green dress, it had been attended to by the invisible hotel fairies. His shirt was pressed and spotless, his trousers immaculate. He'd shaved—lost that sexy two-day relaxed traveller stubble.

It was like winding the clock back to the moment she'd first seen him. He was all imposing, intimidating businessman. And so out of her league.

'Let's go,' he said starkly.

She just nodded.

On the long drive back to Melbourne he was silent, his thoughts no doubt consumed with his upcoming meeting. There was nothing she could do to ease that stress for him. Coming over all 'Steffi Leigh' chirpy wasn't going to help. Her own anxiety was rising anyway. There'd been no message from Tara this morning, and still nothing at all from Dan.

She felt terrible for going two days without talking to her brother. She'd always promised herself that she wouldn't be like her mum. Wouldn't let her feelings for a guy get in the way of what was really important. She would never forget her family.

But hadn't she done just that? Walking out with no warning for two days? For a decadent sexual tryst?

She had to get back to Dan. She had to know he was okay. She tried not to let Jack see her agitation. He had enough to worry about.

'*Still* with the phone?' He finally broke his silence with a weak tease. 'It hasn't left your hand since we left the Green Veranda.'

'Playing catch-up.' She shrugged. 'You know how it is.'

'Yeah,' he sighed. 'Damn it, I can't believe I slept so late.' He glanced at his watch again. 'Is it okay with you if we go to the meeting first? Then I'll drop you home. I can get a taxi from your place and leave the car with you—I know you don't really want to drive it.'

'I'll be fine driving it in town. Go to the meeting, then we can go straight to the hotel. I'm in no hurry to get home,' she lied.

'Okay. Sure.' He paused. 'Do you mind waiting for me?'

'Not at all.'

She was too close to admitting she'd wait for him for ever if he asked.

Too lame. Too much like her mother. The sooner she got away from him the better.

Jack couldn't believe he'd slept in—that he'd been able to get into such a relaxed state before today of all days.

It was a miracle. And she was sitting right beside him. But she was texting again—furiously. There was no hiding her furtiveness as she checked for messages. Suspicion shot cold arrows into his gut. He had the feeling she wasn't being entirely open with him again, but he didn't have time to talk with her now.

As he pulled into the car park of his birth father's office building his hands felt cold and slippery and his heart raced, making him breathless.

Stupid to be so nervous. What could this matter? He was happy, he had a great life—great family, great job, great sex-life if and when he wanted it.

'I shouldn't be long,' he said vaguely. 'I don't think…'

He didn't know how long he was going to be. He didn't even know how he was going to bring the subject up, and he'd had all his life to imagine the meeting. What was he going to do? Walk up and say, *Hi, Dad*?

For the first time in his life he felt afraid even to move. *Harden up.*

The reality couldn't be worse than anything he'd imagined in all these years. But he still couldn't move.

'Jack?' She'd unclipped her seatbelt and leaned across the passenger seat. Now she turned his face towards her with her gentle hand. She smiled a half-smile at him. 'It'll be okay.'

She didn't know that. Nor did he. But looking into her eyes made him feel better anyway.

'Who knows?' she added softly. 'You guys might become great friends and you'll find yourself coming back to Melbourne all the time. Then you'll find my lists super-useful.' She winked—total Steffi Leigh.

He smiled. Come back to Melbourne all the time?

He'd get to see her.

He drew in a deep breath and energy flooded into his heart. She moved to sit back but he stopped her—cupping the back of her head and drawing her close again. He looked into her blue-green guileless eyes and kissed her.

Her soft lips parted…her tongue met his. Her whole body responded and the tension in his own body eased.

That was what he'd needed. Her touch. *Her.*

He got out of the car without another word and walked towards the squat building that was the headquarters for the construction company Darren Thompson owned, smiling to himself.

Yeah, he could cope with seeing more of Stephanie Johnson.

As the automatic doors slid shut behind him he looked back at the car. He could see her sitting in the passenger seat, her head bent as she looked at her phone. Frantically tapping out messages again.

He laughed to himself, then turned, choosing to take the stairs rather than the elevator because he had adrenalin to burn.

On the third floor the receptionist smiled and welcomed him.

He was used to people waiting for him—welcoming him. So far, so normal. Maybe it was going to be okay.

He didn't have to wait long to find out. After only a moment the receptionist escorted him to an office at the end of the corridor.

Darren Thompson had risen to stand behind his somewhat messy desk. He was only an inch or so shorter than Jack. He had dark hair, streaked with grey. His eyes were a different colour, though.

Jack knew he had his mother's eyes.

'Jack Wolfe—CEO of Wolfe Enterprises. What brings you to my little empire?' Darren gestured towards an empty chair on the other side of his desk before sitting again. 'You want to start putting up buildings?'

So he'd done a little research on him? Jack would have too. But Darren couldn't know the real reason for his visit—Jack's adoption had been kept very private.

'I've not come here about a business matter.' Jack couldn't sit. He paced, walking over to the window. He could see the pale yellow car in the car park. He almost smiled. Instead he took a breath and turned back to face his father. 'I was adopted by the Wolfe family. My birth mother was Lisa Kelly. I was born on July nineteenth, twenty-eight years ago.'

Darren didn't move. 'Why is this of any relevance to me?'

'Because in the year prior to my birth *you* were my mother's boyfriend.'

The man looked up at him for a long time. Saying nothing.

'I believe you're my birth father,' Jack finally added when the silence had become too pointed.

He didn't want to believe it. His investigator's report hadn't made for pleasant reading. Darren Thompson was known for poor business practices, shocking employee relations and a suspicious private life. He'd been picked up by the police for 'male assaults female' but the woman—his fiancée at the time—had refused to press charges.

Jack had wanted to meet Darren and make his own assessment, and he was reading the man's body language now...

'No blood test is one hundred per cent accurate.' Darren's mouth barely moved as he spoke. 'I'll never accept you as my son.'

*Wow.* Just like that. Jack's blood ran so cold it almost congealed.

'You want money?' Darren asked. 'Is that why you've made this up?'

*Seriously?*

'I'm Jack Wolfe,' Jack answered, as coolly as he could. 'If you know anything about Wolfe Enterprises you know I have no need for money.'

'Just because they gave you their name doesn't mean they're giving you their cash, though, does it?' his father sneered. 'So many of these things are just for the look of it. Softening the ruthless business empire image by adopting some druggie chick's abandoned kid.'

'My mother didn't abandon me.'

She'd *chosen* his future. And his personal story hadn't ever been in the press. The Wolfes had never tried to use their adoption of him for commercial gain.

'No? She was addicted to cash and anything else I gave her. We were doing okay for a while, but then she told me she was pregnant.' The man rolled his eyes. 'How do I know you're mine? She could've been screwing half the town for all I know. In fact I reckon she was. She'd do it with anyone who could get her a fix. She always dressed too tarty and talked too friendly. I had to sort her out.'

'Sort her out?' Jack asked icily.

The man admitted nothing more. He looked Jack over. 'I told her to have an abortion, but she ran off.'

Of course she had. Because this bastard was a bully who'd probably threatened to beat her—to 'sort her out' again. And why had he taken it upon himself to 'sort her out'? Because a man was the boss of a woman? A man decided what she did or didn't do? A man decreed what a woman should and shouldn't wear? Told her what to do with her body? With her baby?

His mother must have been terrified, given she'd run so far. And she'd never once looked back. She'd never returned to this country. And now Jack knew why. Now he knew part of the reason why she'd turned to artificial stimulants to help her get through her days.

Bile burned its way up from his gut, tasting foul in the back of his throat.

'Thanks for your time.' Jack turned and walked towards the door.

He refused to apologise for interrupting him.

Refused to apologise for being born.

Less than thirty seconds and it was all over. Every bit as bad as his worst imaginings.

'Jack.'

Jack froze. He hated it that the man had called him by his first name. But he swivelled and looked back.

Darren had risen, a calculating gleam in his eye. 'You're really CEO of that travel book company?'

'Yes,' Jack said stiffly. 'I really am.'

'Huh…' Darren tugged at his collar. 'You know, you took me by surprise just then. Maybe we should spend some time together. Get to know each other.'

The man had no redeeming qualities at all. He was *worse* than Jack's worst imaginings. Because not only was he a bully, he was also only interested in someone if they could be of benefit to him in some way—*financially.*

'I don't think we need to,' Jack answered. 'I think we're done.'

He got out of the office and ran down the stairs before he fell down.

No wonder his mother had run away to the other side of the world—to Indonesia. Then to America. No wonder his parents had always claimed not to know anything. They'd wanted to protect him from that jerk of a man. A guy who wanted everything his way and didn't care how he got it. And what did that mean for Jack? What had *he* inherited from the pair of them?

Nature versus nurture was a debate that had raged for years. But there was no doubting all those 'separated twin' studies that showed how dominant DNA was. Even though some of those twins grew up in families miles apart, in both distance and opportunities, so many still turned out similar.

Genetic predisposition was undeniable.

Jack paused just outside the building and looked over at the pastel yellow car.

Hadn't he questioned Stephanie's choice of clothing only the day before? Hadn't he ordered freaking clothes *for* her? And hadn't he given her few real choices?

He'd been beyond controlling. Hadn't he effectively bullied her into staying with him?

He'd seduced her that first night, teasing her on the bonnet of the car until she hadn't been able to say anything but yes. He'd wanted her. And he'd done everything he could think of to have her. He'd been thinking of nothing but himself—his own desires.

He'd been utterly selfish.

But she'd agreed. She'd stayed. She would have said no if she'd really wanted to, right?

But doubt clawed deep. Why else would she have stayed with him?

Because she wanted him to buy her blog.

Acknowledging the truth hurt. So much.

Stupid to have had hope. Stupid to have wanted to know. Stupid to let someone get close enough to hurt you.

Had she been going along with him simply because of her need to sell the blog? She'd said what had happened between them personally wasn't to be related to the deal, but how could it not be? Had she given herself to him because she'd thought she had to?

Had he abused her in that way?

He'd thought she was strong. But now he thought back to her bitten fingernails. Her nerves. Her lack of sophistication once that make-up had been washed off her face. And all the while he'd been sure she was still holding something back from him.

He checked his phone and saw he'd missed a bunch of calls. And then, even as he was staring at it, it vibrated in his hand. He didn't recognise the number. Which was weird, because his PA *never* gave his number out.

'Hello?' he answered brusquely, still not walking towards Stephanie in the car.

'Is that Jack Wolfe?'

'Yes.'

'This is Tara.'

'Tara?' Steffi Leigh's sidekick—the make-up diva who liked hand cream?

'I'm trying to get hold of Steffi—is she still with you?'

'She's just in the car.' His bloodless heart began to hammer. 'Can I help?'

'It's Dan.'

There was a problem with her kitten? 'What's wrong with him?'

'I can't get hold of him. I knocked on the door 'til my knuckles bled but he didn't answer. I left my key there yesterday, when I had a go at him, and now I can't get in.'

Jack was momentarily confused. 'How's a cat going to answer the door?'

'Cat? I'm talking about Dan. Her brother.'

The sports star? Jack frowned. Wasn't he off at college on a scholarship or something?

'I'm sure he's in there—he never leaves,' Tara added. 'God, I'm so worried—'

'Slow down, Tara, and tell it to me slowly.' His brain was already scrambled and he wasn't making sense of this.

'I thought it would do him good to tough it out for a couple days. He takes such advantage of her. I thought some time out might help him appreciate all she does.'

In what way did her brother take advantage of her?

'She's basically been a house hostage for a year and a half. You take her away for two days and he does this. It's awful.'

'Tara, stop babbling and tell me what the problem is.'

'I had a go at him for being so hard on her and then I left him to it. And now he's not answering the door. Or the phone. And I'm scared.'

'And you're worried he's done something?'

'Yeah. Should I call the police? An ambulance?'

'What's wrong with him?'

'She didn't tell you?' Tara drew in a sharp breath. 'Now she's going to kill me.'

He tried to speak calmly. 'She's not going to kill you.'

'I can't believe she didn't tell you...' Tara was speaking breathlessly again. 'Actually, I can. God, she's *so* pig-headed.'

'Tara!' he snapped. 'What the hell is wrong with him?'

There was a split second of utter silence. Then he heard her take a breath.

'Dan got meningitis about eighteen months ago,' Tara said dully. 'He had an arm and a leg amputated. He should be managing better now, but he lives like an invalid and is totally dependent on Steffi. And now he's not answering the phone or the door.'

'Where's her apartment?' Jack snapped.

He rapidly searched on his phone when Tara gave him the address, frowning when he realised it was in a housing block on the edge of an industrial development. Hardly the chic city apartment you'd think Steffi Leigh would have.

'We can be there quickly. We're not that far from there now.'

He listened as Tara gave him more detailed directions. But he was so shocked he could hardly think.

'So *that's* why she wants to sell the blog,' he muttered, more to himself than to Tara, as he started striding towards the car. 'Of *course*. She's slaving for her brother, who just sits on the sofa making constant demands on her. She has no life. Limited money. I mean, she gets *some* income from ads, but she won't sell out and do full-on product placement, and it's not like she can eat the beauty samples she gets sent...'

So with an invalid brother she had to take care of there was no way Stephanie would have said no to Jack.

He felt sick.

He understood it all now. The reason for her determination to smile, no matter how snarky he'd got when they'd first met. The reason she'd been so afraid his finding out that she had assistance would put him off any kind of purchase.

'This is why you help?' he asked Tara.

'Of course. Other friends send her info for the blog too. She verifies it as best she can, then goes for it. But she can't keep doing it. She needs a life of her own.'

'What does she want to do?'

Tara's pause was shorter this time. But still pointed. 'Didn't you talk to her *at all*?'

Well, *he* had talked. He'd spilled his guts. He'd thought she'd opened up to him and he'd opened up to her and there'd been a bond between them—something more than sexual.

But she hadn't opened up at all.

She hadn't trusted or cared enough to tell him everything. She'd been *afraid* to.

And that hurt him bitterly.

'Look, this is wasting time,' Tara said. 'I need to talk to her.'

'I'll get her to call you in a minute.'

'Great. Tell her I'm sorry. I'm so, *so* sorry.'

He was the one who was sorry.

And so freaking *angry*.

# CHAPTER TEN

SHE HADN'T HEARD from Tara and she couldn't get hold of Dan because her stupid phone battery had died.

Stephanie glanced up at the building where Jack had gone to meet his father, hoping it was going okay. He'd looked so vulnerable and her heart ached for him too much. She was far too worried about it for her own good, because this was only a two-day fling.

Except it felt like so much more.

The way he'd teased her and then laughed with her… the lengths he'd gone to to ensure her pleasure… Not just in bed but in seeing that echidna, going to that restaurant, playing in the pool…in taking the time to just *be* with her.

But she was making too much of it, right? She hadn't been with anyone like this *ever*. She was making more where there was actually nothing.

Just a good time.

He was going back to America once this meeting was over. She was one holiday fling of who knew how many? All humour—no hearts.

She'd known that. She'd walked into this with her eyes wide open.

But last night… She drew in a deep breath as she remembered the way he'd talked. The way he'd looked at her. *That* had felt like something more. He'd opened up. He'd told her so much and she'd ached to do the same. But there was no point in telling him about Dan now. Not when he was so stressed about meeting his father. Not when there was still the blog deal to discuss later. There was no reason for him to know the truth about her brother. He probably wouldn't be bothered about something that was only personal to *her*.

She had to face reality—sooner rather than later.

She wasn't the kind of woman a man like him would settle with even if he *did* decide to settle some time. He'd go for some model-type or a celebrity. She'd seen the girlfriends his brother George had had—he was always in the online gossip columns with yet another model or actress or singer. Or maybe Jack would go for an ultra-brainy, Girl Friday travelling type...

Either way, she wasn't it.

But in her heart there was that whispering temptation, that bewitching fantasy. If he asked she'd drop everything and run off with him. She'd follow him to the four corners of the world in a heartbeat.

And she *hated* that weakness within herself.

She couldn't be the kind of woman who dropped everything for a new man. She couldn't do what her mother had done. She hadn't cared enough to stick around and help her own children. Not even when Dan had been so unwell. And that hurt. She could never shirk her responsibilities in that way. Or give up her own career for something that wasn't even love.

And she couldn't leave Australia anyway because Dan needed her. Until he was happier and more sorted she had to be there for him.

And she had to know he was okay now. If only her stupid phone battery had lasted another couple of hours...

The driver's door suddenly opened and Jack got into the car.

'That was quick,' she said. 'Are you okay?'

He didn't look okay. His face was pale and his jaw was tight and he was staring ahead. Too determinedly *not* looking at her.

He put the key in the ignition and started the car, yanked his seatbelt on and pulled out of the car park.

'Jack?' Stephanie scrambled to put on her own seatbelt. Then, curling her suddenly clammy hands into fists on her lap, she sent him a sideways look. 'You don't want to talk about it?'

'As much as *you* want to talk about your invalid brother.'

She froze. He knew about Dan? Since when? Had he been waiting all this time for her to mention it?

'How do you know?' she asked.

'Tara called.'

*Tara* had told him about Dan? Why would she have done that when Stephanie had gone to such lengths to ensure he *didn't* know?

She stared down at her dead phone, a horrible cold feeling seeping under her skin.

Jack tossed his phone into her lap. 'You'd better call her.'

Her heart went from zero to three hundred in a split second. Her stomach roiled. But she picked up his phone and tapped in Tara's number.

'Steffi?' Tara asked as soon as she answered.

'What's happened?' Stephanie could barely speak her throat was so constricted. 'Is he okay?'

'I don't know.' Tara sounded near to tears. 'I can't get hold of him. He's not answering the phone. Not answering the door… I'm here right now and he won't answer. Shall I get the building caretaker to open up?'

'When did you last see him?'

'Lunchtime yesterday,' Tara mumbled.

'But when you texted last night you said he was fine.' Stephanie couldn't understand it. 'Didn't you see him?'

Dan hadn't replied to a single one of the texts she'd sent him.

'I thought it would do him some good to see how much he takes you for granted…'

'You left him *alone*?' Stephanie snapped. 'You know he's not…he's not…'

He couldn't cope with being alone. Not for that long.

'He's perfectly okay.' Tara suddenly fought back. 'He could manage a lot better than he does. He takes advantage of you—'

'He's my *brother*,' Stephanie interrupted. 'And I trusted you.' Her emotions threatened to better her and she spoke more quickly. 'I'm on my way. Just wait for me.'

She ended the call and stared straight ahead. She realised that somehow Jack knew the way to her home. That he must know much more than he'd let on. And she felt dreadful.

'Not a cat, then, huh?' Jack asked.

She'd lied to him. And he was mad about it. 'I didn't think it was something we needed to talk about…' she muttered.

His laugh was short and a little bitter—and finite.

'It was nothing to do with the blog,' she tried to explain. 'Or the deal—'

'I get it,' he interrupted shortly. 'Don't worry about it.'

But she *was* worried. She was worried every which way—for Dan, for Tara, for herself…and there was a hurt deep within her for Jack. She didn't even know if it had gone okay with his father.

But he wasn't in a talking mood.

And she shouldn't be thinking of anyone but her brother and the hell he might be in right now.

She picked up Jack's phone again and rang her home number. There was no answer. She left a message asking Dan to answer. Then she redialled. And redialled. And redialled.

Dan was all that mattered.

This thing with Jack had been a mistake. He was going back to America and he'd be gone from her life. It was ending now anyway. It would be like ripping off a plaster. Quick and painless.

Only it was never painless.

Her anxiety was painful to watch. Jack glanced sideways as he drove along the route Tara had given him.

Stephanie nibbled on her fingernails as she repeatedly dialled her home number. There was never any answer. He could sense her willing him to drive faster. He did—as safely and quickly as he could. And in silence he waited, giving her the chance to tell him something about it. Anything.

She didn't take it.

She had never been truly interested.

He got it that she presented a façade to the blog world— that online she showed only part of herself: 'Steffi Leigh'— but the thought that she'd maintained most of that façade with *him*, when he'd really thought she hadn't... When he'd opened up to her... When he'd thought they'd shared something deeper, as if she'd felt the same kind of emotional connection that he had...

What a joke.

It was a relief when he pulled up to her apartment building. But painful when she turned to look at him.

'I...' Her voice trailed off as she glanced up at the building.

Her breath came quickly, panicked.

But she couldn't look him in the eye. Didn't know what to say. Clearly she didn't want him to come in with her to ensure all was okay.

*Too freaking bad.*

As if he was going to leave her alone to face whatever hell was up there...

He got out of the car and marched round the front of it to open the passenger door for her.

She stepped out onto the footpath without a word. He saw her stand taller, squaring her shoulders.

'Okay, then…' She glanced back at him. 'Thank—'

'I'm coming up with you. Don't think for a second that you're going to stop me.'

And if that made him a bully all over again, so be it.

Stephanie took one look into his hard face and knew there was no arguing with him. Much as she wanted to. But she wanted to see Dan more than anything else right now. He had to come first.

So she ignored Jack and marched into the building. There she ignored the elevator and sprinted up the stairs to the sixth floor.

Tara was waiting nervously on the landing.

'I am *so* sorry,' she said, rushing up to her.

'Don't.' Stephanie shook her head and waved her back. 'We'll talk later. I just need to make sure he's okay.'

Her hands shook as she unlocked the door.

'Dan?' she called out as it finally swung open. 'Dan? Where are you?'

There was no answer. She ran down the small narrow hall, glancing through the doorway on the left. He wasn't in his bedroom.

'Dan?'

The curtains were closed in the lounge, stopping the sun from streaming in and brightening the room. She had the feeling they hadn't been opened at all in the couple of days she'd been gone.

Her brother lay on the sofa in an ancient pair of trackies and a stained tee shirt. Cartoons were playing on the television. He finally dragged his gaze from the garish colours flickering on the screen and looked up at her.

'Did you get more of those corn chips?'

For a moment Stephanie just gaped. Then she drew

breath. 'Tara has been banging on the door for *ages*. And calling. *I've* been calling. Why are you ignoring the phone?' The handset was there on the sofa—*next* to him.

She took in the sulky line of her younger brother's mouth and knew. He'd *chosen* not to answer. He'd *deliberately* set out to worry her.

And she was so very angry with him.

'You went all drama queen because you were out of *corn chips*?'

'I like corn chips,' he answered.

'I was away, having a nice time for the first time in...' She couldn't finish that sentence. 'You *resent* me for that?'

'You just disappeared,' he grumbled.

'Tara called to check on you.'

'Tara's mean.'

'And you're a spoilt little—'

'Tara, don't.' Stephanie turned to interrupt her friend before she made things worse. 'You go. We'll talk later.'

Tara looked reluctant, and she glared at Dan as she walked out. 'Call me when you need me,' she said to Stephanie.

But Stephanie didn't want to need anyone. *Ever.*

And then Jack stepped away from where he'd been leaning against the back wall.

Stephanie gaped. For those couple of minutes she'd forgotten he'd followed her up here. And now she looked around her apartment and saw what he must be seeing. The chipped mismatched crockery on the mess-covered coffee table in front of Dan. The ancient stained lounge suite he was sprawling on. The total lack of anything beautiful or pristine.

Nothing like the life *he* was used to, with his swanky hotels and fancy restaurants and unlimited funds.

And no doubt he'd glanced through her bedroom doorway on his way in and seen that one pretty corner and the rest a bare mess of not very much.

'Steffi Leigh' was nothing. *Had* nothing.

'Stephanie,' he said. 'Can I—?'

'No,' she snapped, suddenly angrier and more humiliated than she'd ever been in her life. He looked so damn incongruous there, in his perfect freaking suit. Made of money, wasn't he? Hell, one of his shoes alone had probably cost more than their lounge suite. 'Do you mind giving us some privacy?'

His expression froze. His eyes were so dark they were like cold coal. Only they burned right through to her bones.

'As you can see, everything is fine.' She gritted the words out. 'I'm sorry you were dragged up here.'

She was sorry he'd seen it all. Every last bit of her not so Steffi Leigh life.

She stalked back down the hallway, assuming he'd follow her. And he did.

'Stephanie—'

'No,' she said again, opening her front door. She recognised that tone of his—implacable, determined. But she wasn't going to give in to it this time. She wasn't going to take anything more from him. 'If I don't need help from my best friend, I certainly don't need help from *you*.'

He looked angry. 'So afraid of letting someone help, aren't you? Which is kind of ironic when apparently you're sacrificing your life to look after your brother. But maybe that's just an excuse to avoid really living. Maybe you use him as your excuse to hide away inside, where you can maintain your Steffi Leigh online fantasy of fun and perfection. Because you're too afraid to let someone in.'

She very nearly slapped him. Because she *had* let him in.

'Right.' She nodded. 'Whereas *you* spend your life running away from your problems. *Escaping.*' Scathingly she used his favourite word. 'Using work as your excuse not to give anyone—family, friend, lover—more than two days of your precious time.'

He jerked as if she *had* slapped him.

'Right,' he nodded, mimicking her smart tone. 'I'll get going, then, and fulfil your low expectations of me.'

But as he walked away her heart lurched. She remembered just what he'd been through. 'What about—?'

'The blog?' he interrupted, turning his head, his sharp eyes stabbing. 'It's all about personality,' he said curtly. 'Things on the internet always are. Personality can't be replicated. *You* are your blog. And, as you once said, you're not on the table. You cannot be bought.'

'That's right,' she said softly. 'I can't.'

He was right about everything.

She had been afraid to let him in. And she couldn't let herself take from him now. She couldn't let herself rely on him. Because then she'd give him *everything*. And *do* anything he asked of her. And she refused to be that weak.

She hadn't been going to ask about the blog just then. She'd been going to ask about his father. But why would he want to talk to her about that now? He just wanted to escape again. And fair enough.

'Okay, then,' she said icily as he continued to glare at her. But there was still that last shred of dignity, of politeness, within her. She held the door and as he finally walked through it murmured, 'Thank—'

'Bye.' He cut her off and walked away.

She slammed the door. Bolted it. Then closed her eyes to hold back the tears.

It was five minutes before she was under enough control to walk back to her brother in the lounge. He'd moved from sprawling to actually sitting, but she couldn't bring herself to sit down next to him.

'What were you *thinking*?' she asked him. 'Why didn't you just answer the damn phone?'

He looked mutinous.

'You wanted me to feel guilty? You wanted me to pay?' Her eyes filled. 'For how long do I have to pay, Dan?' Because right now it felt as if she was going to have to pay for ever. 'It wasn't my fault.' As guilty as she felt, she knew that it hadn't been.

'I know that,' he snapped, goaded. 'But you're always so *busy*.'

'I'm always *here*,' she argued.

'Staring at your computer screen.'

'Because I'm trying to make us some money. Because we have to eat.'

'You'll *never* understand what it's like for me!' he shouted suddenly.

'No.' She paused, counting to ten, trying so hard not to shout back. Or to cry. 'I probably won't. And you know what? I can't fix it for you either. I've tried for so long. I've tried everything I can think of to make it better. And I can't.'

She lost the battle against her tears.

'*You* have to rebuild your life, Dan. I can help you, support you, but this has to come from *you*. There's nothing more I can say. Or do. I don't know how to reach you. How to help you. I've tried and I've failed.' She shook her head and turned away from him. 'I'm done.'

She walked into her bedroom and closed the door. She looked at the 'Steffi Leigh' corner. Its bright and stylish decor mocked her—its perfect façade so far removed from reality. A fake—a failure, in every way.

She fell onto the bed face-down, pressing her eyes into the pillow so she wouldn't have to see any of it.

'The airport, please.' Jack instructed the taxi driver, avoiding the urge to go back to her and grovel out an apology.

The other urge riding him was stronger—to get the hell on the road.

Keep moving. Keep working. Keep safe.

He needed to be alone. He always had. And it would be better for Stephanie. She had trouble enough without having to deal with the current emotional mess that he was.

She didn't want his help—she couldn't have made that clearer. She'd cut him off. Pushed him away with words and her manner alone.

And he'd retaliated in kind. He knew how to put up walls and end a conversation. Because the last thing he'd wanted to hear was her *gratitude*—pure platitude that it was.

He boarded a jet that afternoon and on the long flight back to the States watched six movies. He couldn't remember the titles of any the second he disembarked from the plane.

Los Angeles—city of dreams and destiny for some.

He didn't even make it out of the terminal before his curiosity—his need—got the better of him. He pulled out his tablet and hooked into the WiFi, flicked to her blog. She hadn't uploaded anything new since she'd met him, so he watched her most recent performance again.

Now he understood why she was so brittle. And he couldn't believe that her fans couldn't see it—that behind that perky demeanour and the bright smile of her most recent posting there was sadness. There was worry in those revealing eyes.

Steffi Leigh was a part of Stephanie, but only one part. On screen she was one-dimensional, but there was so much more to her.

He'd been wrong in what he'd said to her. She *wanted* adventures. She *wanted* to travel. That was why she'd been so excited when his PA had made initial overtures about her blog. Because she wasn't able to leave. Because she was caring for her brother and doing everything she could to stay afloat.

No wonder she'd looked so enchanted by the beauty of the forest and had been so enthusiastic and open in her enjoyment of that restaurant. When was the last time she'd eaten out?

And she'd been using all that make-up to cover up the sadness. Forcing herself to be 'Steffi Leigh' because it had become more than a fun blog with her schoolfriends—it had become a job. It had become a source of income and a possible springboard to something more.

He was flooded with the urge to scoop her up and carry her off for a billion more adventures. He'd take her to a different restaurant every night. Show her all the sights he loved. Share everything with her.

Except that was the last thing she wanted from him. And that was why he'd lashed out at her in the apartment.

Because he knew she'd only gone to the Green Veranda with him because she'd been desperate to sell the blog. She'd not wanted to say no to him. And, while she'd enjoyed the surroundings, he could no longer believe that she'd enjoyed *him*.

He'd thought she'd opened up to him. But she hadn't. She hadn't told him the most important thing of all. She'd let him use her because she'd thought she had to. And he was still so angry, so hurt about that. But he wanted her to be set free so she wouldn't ever have to pretend with anyone else.

She wouldn't accept help from him personally—he got that. But in business…? Maybe he had a chance.

# CHAPTER ELEVEN

IN FROZEN SILENCE Stephanie stared at the email.

Jack had made an offer for her blog. It was there in black and white. With no reference to the few days they'd shared together.

She phoned Tara. 'I've had an email from Jack Wolfe.'

'Is it a decent amount?'

'You *know* about the offer?' Steph frowned. Why didn't Tara sound surprised?

'I… I think he'd be crazy not to want to take the blog over.'

'Tara, what aren't you telling me?' Then she got it. 'You've spoken with him again? How could you *do* that?' Panic rose within her—what secrets had her friend told him this time?

'How could you *not*?'

Because he hadn't got in touch. Until now. And now it was a sparsely worded three-sentence offer to buy her blog for a ridiculous amount of money.

'It wasn't right to contact him. It was only ever about business.'

'Right. That's why you slept with him.'

'I didn't want him to make an offer from pity. I didn't want to be a charity case.' And that was exactly what she'd become.

'Steffi, stop undervaluing yourself. That's *not* why he's offering to buy the blog.'

Of course it was. He didn't need the blog. This offer

was only because of what he'd seen. Because of what he thought he knew.

'Have you accepted it?' Tara asked.

'What do *you* think?' Stephanie muttered. She'd turned him down, of course. In a sparsely worded two-sentence email.

'I'm sorry.' Tara sighed. 'I didn't realise you'd be so hurt. You want me to come round?'

'No, I'm fine. Truly. I'm sorry for getting upset.'

'It's okay to get upset,' Tara said softly. 'I'm sorry it's all been such a mess.'

Steph hung up the phone and wiped away yet another stupid tear. She shouldn't be this hurt. She'd known him for only a smidgeon more than forty-eight hours. This was infatuation. *Pathetic*.

But it was the possibility…the promise. The *potential* of what they'd had.

And the passion.

That could never be replicated. And a lifetime wouldn't be long enough to exhaust it. He was seared on her heart. And she was every bit as much of a fool as her mum.

'Stephanie?'

*Oh, hell*. She wiped her cheeks again and turned in her chair to face her brother.

He stood in the doorway, awkwardly leaning on his crutch.

'I'm sorry I've been such a jerk.' He cleared his throat. 'But…uh… I guess I'm scared.'

Surprised, she stilled. 'Of what?'

'Everything. Even getting out through the front door. I just…feel scared of everything.'

'I'm scared too,' she whispered.

He looked at her. 'Of what?'

'Everything.'

He hopped into the room and sat on the end of her bed.

'I thought you weren't going to come back. That you were going to leave. Like Mum.'

'I'd *never* do that,' she whispered, horrified. 'She left me too.'

'She left you with me. Which is worse in a way.'

'No, it's not!' She half laughed, half cried. 'I *love* you, Dan.'

'It's not just because of me that you're crying, is it?'

Her brother looked at her. The protective expression on his face melted the last of her anger with him.

'It's that guy. Mr Steroids-in-a-Suit.'

'That was just business.'

Dan looked as if he didn't believe her. 'I heard what he said. About you using me to hide from life.'

She closed her eyes. 'It isn't true.'

'I think it is. You've given up so much for me,' Dan mumbled. 'And I think I've been hiding too. Using you.' He dropped his head. 'You should have the *best* guy, Stephanie—only the best. And he should know how amazing you are. And if he doesn't—'

'If he doesn't?' she interrupted with a watery laugh.

'I'll punch him.'

Steph laughed. Her brother laughed too. They both laughed until they cried. And then they sobered.

'I'm sorry.' Her brother wrapped his good arm around her.

'So am I.' She leaned her head on his shoulder. 'We can't go on like this,' she said softly. 'We're both scared. Both lonely. Both treading water—'

'No. You're not. Your blog is amazing.'

'It's stupid.'

'No, it's not.'

'It's fake.'

'It's *you*.'

'It's one very small bit of me. Not the real me.'

'Then *make* it the real you,' he said simply. 'It used to be.'

Show the rest of the room? That was what Jack had said. But the filters were there to protect herself and her brother.

'What do *you* want to do?' she asked him.

He sighed. 'I know you're right. I need to do something. Study something. Travel, even. I can't live staying scared like this. It's more crippling than the loss of my leg. And I can't keep you trapped either. You have to go too. We both have to walk on our own again.'

'Dan…' She sniffed. 'I'm so sorry.'

'It wasn't your fault, Steffi.' He cuddled her closer. 'It was just fate.' He breathed out. 'I don't want you to leave,' he muttered. 'But I don't want to hold you back either. So I'm going to find a residential programme.'

'You don't have to do that.' A tear fell from her cheek.

'I *do* have to,' he said roughly. 'If I don't I'll just get stuck here again, and you'll stay with me because you're loyal, and I'll hold us both back. I won't do that any more.' His chest rose and fell quickly.

He was braver than her, she realised. Because now it came to it she was terrified. Jack had been right—she'd been using Dan as a safety blanket to keep her heart safe.

'I'm going to miss you.'

'We'll see each other lots. It won't be easy. I'm sure I'll have grumpy moments.'

'You're going to do great.' She wiped her eyes with the back of her hand and drew in a huge breath. 'We both are.'

Try as hard as he could, Jack couldn't find a comfortable seat in the first-class lounge at the airport. His phone burned in his hand.

Finally he gave in—only he dialled the number second on the list.

'Jack?' His mother answered right away and sounded worried. 'Where are you?'

'LA. At the airport.'

He had been for the last couple of hours, while he waited for Stephanie to reply to his offer. He'd thought she'd be quick about it, given she was all but surgically attached to her phone. And while he was waiting he felt unable to board the plane for the next leg of the journey.

'Are you okay? We've been trying to reach you but your PA said you'd gone AWOL in Australia.'

He heard the anxiety in his mother's voice. She knew that something was wrong. And he couldn't hold it back— couldn't think of a way to soften it.

'I went there to find my birth father. Succeeded.'

There was a moment of silence.

'Oh, Jack. How did you…? Why didn't you…?'

He winced, hating hearing her pain. 'I'm sorry,' he said softly.

'*Why?*' his mother asked, her voice rallying. 'You can't be sorry. If we'd known we'd have helped you. You should have told—' She suddenly broke off. 'Was it okay?'

'No…' he murmured, leaning forward to press the heel of his hand to his forehead, hiding his face from the world. 'It wasn't. But you knew it wasn't going to be okay, didn't you?'

'Oh, no, Jack,' his mother whispered. 'I never wanted it to be like that.'

'When I was a kid, every time I mentioned him… asked…you changed the subject. You looked worried.'

He felt his anger building over that old sense of powerlessness.

'I was worried!' she cried. 'We didn't know anything much. And for a long time I was terrified he'd turn up and try to take you away from us. I never wanted to lose you. But I never wanted to drive you away.'

'You haven't, Mom.' Now he felt even worse.

'What happened?'

'He's a bastard. He doesn't want to know me. Never did. He asked her to get rid of me.'

'Oh, Jack. Your mother was strong. So strong to get away from all that. But in the end she felt she couldn't cope alone. She knew we loved you. That we could give you everything she didn't think she could. But all her love was for *you*, Jack. She adored you. And she tried so hard to keep you herself.'

He knew that. In his head he understood. But somehow it still hurt. *Why* couldn't she have fought harder for him? *Why* couldn't she have straightened herself out and been stronger?

And as for Darren Thompson...? That bruise was too fresh. Too raw.

'Jack?' His father had come on the line. 'Son, where are you? We'll come get you. I always suspected...' His father broke off.

'You never asked about him,' his mother said sadly. 'You hadn't in so long. I thought you were at peace with it. I didn't think it bothered you,' his mother said. 'But of *course* it bothered you.'

He'd not asked because he'd seen their reticence. Their anxiety. But now he realised they'd never spoken of it because he'd *stopped* asking. *He'd* been the one holding back. And then he hadn't told them he was looking because he hadn't wanted to hurt them.

He'd been so afraid—on so many levels.

'Jack?'

'I'm okay. Don't worry.'

Stupid words. He knew his parents were beside themselves right now.

He managed a lame little laugh. 'I'm okay—honest.'

'When are you coming home?' That was his mother again.

'Soon,' he promised. 'I'll call again soon, okay?'

He rang off before they could talk more. Because suddenly he'd realised where he'd gone wrong and he needed time to *think*.

He'd thought having the answers would make his life complete. Would fill that empty little pocket in his heart. Only now that pocket somehow seemed bigger. And it hurt more than it ever had before.

He'd not asked them, not told them how he felt—what he needed to know and why. He'd buried himself in work and closed his worries off from them. Because he'd been stupidly scared. Of their reaction. Really of everything. He'd never realised he was such a coward.

His phone buzzed in his hand and he swiped the screen and held it up to his ear with a wry grin. 'Hey, George.'

'How's your trip panning out?'

Jack knew his mother had called George the second she'd got off the phone to him. The Wolfe clan was rallying. And he loved them for it. Even if talking about it was half killing him.

'It's been…big,' he muttered.

'You need company?'

'No. I'm okay for now. I'll call you when I get to Manhattan.'

Jack glanced down at the tablet on his lap, still on 'The List', and with Steffi Leigh's smiling avatar in the corner. He clicked on the archive and watched her very first vlog. So Steffi, and yet so different. So young—and that giggle…

It tugged his heart.

Tara had her bag of tricks out and the two of them were laughing uncontrollably at the witch's nose Tara had glued wrongly onto Stephanie. It must have been well before her brother's illness. When she'd been excited and full of anticipation, free and happy. Not burdened with responsibility and worry.

He watched the next clip. And the next. So random. So ridiculous. So quirky and cool.

Now he saw why her blog had got so popular. Why it was all those young people liked to tune it. It was fun. *She* was fun.

She'd compiled lists of whatever it was she'd been interested in at the time. And she'd been insatiably curious, insatiably enthusiastic—soaking up new experiences. New places.

But as he worked his way through he saw how it had evolved in the time since Dan's accident. To become more lists, less Steffi.

When he clicked back to the home page he saw she'd posted a new video: 'Three Things to Find in the Rest of the Room'.

'Morning, everyone.'

She was smiling, but she looked so tired and pale.

'I know you've always wondered…what *else* is there? Who's there with Steffi Leigh? Well, you all know Tara, my make-up artist.'

Tara popped her head up alongside Steffi's, waving at the camera.

'She's going to do some more make-up tutorials for you,' Steffi added. 'But the truth is she's also been giving me lots of the info for my lists—as have some of my other friends. Because I've been hanging out at home with my brother, Dan—who's also here with me.'

She turned the camera on her brother. Jack leaned a little closer towards the screen. Dan looked equally pale, but he too was smiling. He was wearing a singlet top and he waved at the camera.

'I'm not going to be posting as much in the next week or so because Dan and I have some personal things we need to do,' Steffi said. 'But I promise there'll be some super-special lists coming up—so be patient…we'll be back with a new segment soon.'

For a second her smile faded and he thought he could see her bruised heart, pinching her features.

'But now…because Tara is here…she's going to show us her best tips for reducing puffy eyes. If you've ever spent a night crying your eyes out, you'll know the kind I mean… see?' She leaned into the camera and laughed—pure Steffi Leigh. With heart. 'Here's how to fix it.'

Why had she had a night crying her eyes out? Was it because of her brother? Because she was pulling back from her blog?

Or was it because of *him*?

His heart thundered and his pulse roared like a dozen motorcycles at the raceway. She was hurting. And he hated it.

He picked up his phone and checked his email. The most recent to land caught his eye. It was from her, and it took him less than a second to read it.

She'd refused his offer.

There was no reference to the time they'd shared together. Just a very polite sentence declining his very generous offer. End of story.

He jumped up from his seat and walked—just for something to do.

Then he caught himself and laughed bitterly. She'd been right in her scathing assessment. He'd been running—escaping—his form of hiding. He'd been using work as his excuse. Travelling all the time. Not giving anyone the chance to get close. Ducking out from risk. From rejection.

But Stephanie was worth that risk, wasn't she?

Somehow—in such a crazily short time—she'd got under his skin. He'd talked to her. He'd let her in. She'd made him want *more*. And, while she might not have opened up to *him*, she'd given him so much. All that emotion in her eyes… No matter how much make-up Tara applied, there was no hiding the hugeness of her heart.

And she'd done the thing he'd challenged her to. She'd turned the camera the other way and shown her less than perfect side. She'd removed the filter and then, as only Steffi Leigh could, she'd given a demo on how to cover up again.

Because everyone needed to cover up sometimes. When they were hurt. When they needed to carry on regardless. It was all in how you did it, right? And who you chose to reveal yourself to.

She'd shown her whole self—and from the number of views the new vlog had already had, and the comments, *so* many people loved Steffi Leigh.

He'd been telling the truth when he'd told her *she* was the blog. People liked *her*. And she might have thought she was putting on a persona, but it was all just a part of her. She was sweet. She was savvy. She was strong.

And she was brave. Far braver than him. She'd taken on so much and she hadn't complained. She'd just got on with it—doing what she thought she had to to survive. And she'd not wanted him to pity her. Or help her. Because she had all the independence and strength that her brother had lost. She had more than enough for the lot of them.

But too much independence could work against you.

She'd said she didn't want to depend on someone too much because she was scared of being like her mum. And scared of being hurt.

He'd never wanted to hurt her. He should have told her that.

How much of her time with him had been a pretence?

Perhaps some of it. Perhaps none.

But he couldn't live the rest of his life without knowing. The thing was, in order to find out he was going to have to open up again. And, yeah, that thought scared him.

Now he realised he'd been holding back all this time. He'd been living half a life.

But now he wanted it all.

# CHAPTER TWELVE

STEPHANIE FROWNED AT the loud knocking on her door. Who was here so crazily early in the morning?

She opened the door and had to count to three before she could think enough to speak.

'Jack…' She breathed out. 'Couldn't sleep?'

He just looked at her, and that was all it took to make her stupid legs go weak.

'I thought you'd left Australia,' she muttered. 'Days ago.'

'I had. But I came back.'

He looked exhausted. Back in jeans and tee and two-day-old stubble and totally gorgeous. But she stopped herself from leaning towards him.

'You mind if I come in for a moment?' he asked.

'Sure, if you'd like to.' She stood back and let him pass.

A small frown flickered over his face before he smoothed it to that bland expression again. She hated the blank look. He was being so polite she wanted to shrivel up and hide behind a rock. There was no warm smile, no wicked look in his eyes. There was no provocative drawl declaring a borderline inappropriate request for a kiss…

He paused just inside the door. 'Is your brother home?'

She shook her head. 'He's away for a couple of days.'

She was so proud of Dan. He was making a push for greater independence and was currently at a clinic, working round the clock with a physio to help him get stronger and feel more comfortable with the prosthetics he'd finally decided to try.

Jack walked a pace behind her to the lounge.

'What happened to him?' he asked.

'Tara didn't tell you?' Stephanie chose one of the two wooden dining chairs.

'Not the whole story,' he answered, taking a seat on the edge of the sofa. 'I want *you* to tell me.'

She hesitated, not really wanting to go there. But not wanting Jack to leave yet either. And maybe she owed him some kind of explanation.

'We went on a holiday together—in the Northern Territory. All my idea. I booked it. I was so excited, I'd wanted to travel for ages.'

She'd sat on the sidelines at all Dan's meets. She'd read or sewed or dreamed up lists. And he'd supported her blog, offering the odd lame-ass suggestion when he thought of one. They'd been close.

They'd needed to be.

'But Dan was tired. He'd had a cold the weekend before, and really he wanted to stay home. But he didn't want me to go on the trip alone. When we were right in the Outback he got this bad headache. Fever. By the time the rash appeared the situation was dire.'

'Meningitis?' Jack said.

Stephanie nodded. 'He almost died. And they had to amputate his lower arm and lower leg.'

'Did your mum fly out to be with you?'

She almost choked on a bitter laugh and shook her head. 'Eventually we flew back to Melbourne—when he was stable enough to make the trip. Mum had avoided the whole drama by having an affair with another new guy. She walked out of her second marriage and straight into the third. She's gone with him to live in France. An absolute passion, she said. A once-in-a-lifetime love. *Again…*'

Jack leaned forward, pressing his hands to his knees. She sensed he was restraining himself from pacing.

'So she's dependent on a guy... Dan's dependent on you... Who do *you* get to depend on?' he asked.

Her heart pounded harder. 'I have my friends—Tara is amazing.'

'But you don't tell her half your problems, do you? You shut her out because she calls things too bluntly for you.' He smiled mirthlessly. 'She's too good a friend.'

'I don't want to bore her. I have other friends. I'm not hopeless. I'm not a pity case.' Stephanie smarted at his judgement.

'I never thought you were.'

'I don't need anyone to look after me.' Her anger sparked now.

'You don't want to be dependent on anyone.' He smiled that rueful smile. 'That's what I used to think about myself... But I've recently decided that I was wrong on that one.'

She wasn't sure she wanted to know any more.

She was the one who jumped up and walked towards the window. 'You came all this way to talk about Dan?'

'Yes, actually.' He leaned back, settling into the old sofa. 'I came back to have the conversation we should have had before I left.'

'About my brother?'

'Yep.'

'What about your father?' She turned, angered by this intrusion into her life. What about *his* life?

'That too.' He looked sombre.

'So what happened?' she asked.

'He was hideous. Every bit as bad as I'd imagined. Didn't want to know me. Dissed my mum. Then at the last minute decided I might be a good business contact after all...'

'Jack...' She cringed inside at his flat, deadened tone. 'I'm sorry...'

'It's okay.' He leaned forward again and rubbed his forehead with the back of his hand. 'I mean, it wasn't like I hadn't imagined something like that… It hurts. Of course it does. Sucks. But I'll be okay. My brothers and my parents have been great. And now I know I can move on.'

That was what he was good at, wasn't it? Moving on.

She swallowed, trying to ease the horrible tightness in her throat. 'So you're travelling soon?' she asked.

'I guess.' He shrugged. 'But first I wanted to apologise to you.'

'For what?'

'For making you go to the Green Veranda with me. Making you stay there when you didn't really want to.'

She blinked. 'You think I didn't really want to go?' A chill trickled down her spine.

'You needed me to buy your blog. Because you needed money for your brother.'

'So you think I didn't really want to do…what we did?' She couldn't believe he'd think that for a second.

And suddenly she was *angry*.

A cautious look sharpened his features, making them more chiselled than ever. 'I'm *trying* to say sorry,' he said tightly.

'For giving me the best few hours of my life?' She marched right up to him, stared down into his upturned face. 'You *regret* it?'

'I regret…how it happened?'

'How *did* it happen?' What was she missing here?

'I seduced you into staying.'

*Oh.* Was that what he thought? 'Do I not have a brain of my own? Could I not have said no?'

He looked confused.

'If I had said no would you have stopped?' she asked.

'Of course.'

'Then what's the problem?' *Of all the stupid things…*

'You don't need to apologise about what happened at the Green Veranda. You need to apologise for—' She broke off.

'What? *What* do I need to be sorry for?' He reached out and grabbed her hips, stopping her from stepping back. 'How have I hurt you?'

She didn't deny that he had. He'd hurt her when he'd ripped her open and then walked away without a glance. And he'd hurt her now.

'You think I prostituted myself? That I only had sex with you because I thought it might help my case?' She jabbed the air with her finger. 'That's ridiculous—I'd *never* do that. If anything, I knew that sleeping with you would jeopardise my chances... But I went ahead and did it anyway because I wanted to. I wanted *you*. I said yes.'

'Only because I made you... There was no real choice.'

'You hardly *forced* me.' She rolled her eyes in frustration. 'If I hadn't wanted to go with you I wouldn't have. If I hadn't wanted to sleep with you I wouldn't have. But I wanted to. I *liked* it.'

Breathing hard, she let her volume reach epic levels.

'And how could I *not* like it? You did everything in your power to please me. You put *my* pleasure ahead of your own. You were *generous*—not selfish. At least physically.'

He'd visibly paled. 'Thank you,' he muttered. 'I'm sorry.'

She drew breath and saw that old lonely look in his eyes. '*Why* are you sorry?' she whispered. 'Why, really?'

'When I was younger I asked my parents about my birth father,' he answered quietly, his hands still holding her hips, keeping her close. 'They said they didn't know anything about him. But I saw the look in their eyes. The worry. The sadness. I've always known it wasn't going to be good. But I needed to know. I *had* to know.'

'Of course you did.' She was unable to stop herself reaching out, raising a hand to his cheek, trying to soothe him.

'But the truth was they *didn't* know—they *weren't* hiding anything from me. They *thought* he must have been abusive…but they didn't know for sure. Turns out he was. He *is*. He's a bully. And I got worried that I'd bullied *you*. That I was like him.'

'Oh, Jack…' Of all the crazy, heartbreaking things.

'And then Tara called and I found out you hadn't told me about your brother. After what we'd shared the night before.' He gazed up at her. 'What I *thought* we'd shared…'

She swallowed, her heart tearing all over again.

'I was hurt,' he whispered. 'To learn you were holding back something so huge. So important. I figured I wasn't at all important to you—I'd clearly made no dent in your defences if you hadn't wanted to tell me something so massive for you.'

'You had enough to deal with,' she whispered.

'So did *you*,' he argued. 'I would've helped.' He looked hurt all over again. 'You told me there was nothing you wanted to escape from and that wasn't true.'

'He's my brother and I love him—I want to help him.' Tears loomed in her eyes and she tried to pull away.

'How come it's okay for you to comfort me but I can't comfort you?' He tugged her back, pulling her closer still, to stand between his spread knees. 'That's not fair, Stephanie. You deserve better than that. And so do I.'

She stilled, stayed in place. 'You want to *comfort* me?'

'Of course I do.'

She couldn't have faith in what she thought she saw in his eyes. She couldn't believe in it. It frightened her too much.

'This is ridiculous,' she muttered. 'We've known each other only a few days—'

'Do you believe in love at first sight?' he interrupted.

She hesitated. Silenced. Scared.

'I do.' He laughed softly. 'Or I sure as hell believe in the possibility. Because I know that the moment I first saw you something clicked within me. There was the *strongest* reaction—physical, for sure. I was attracted. But then I started to get to know you. And what really gets to me is your strength. Your loyalty. Your generosity. I want that for *me*.'

He sighed.

'I've always felt this little gap—right about here.' He pointed to just below his heart. 'Just a little gap at the bottom there. I thought if I found out about my birth father that gap would be filled. That I wouldn't feel that fear any more. Because I'd *know*. Only it worsened. It was *the* worst. But not because of who he was, or what he was like. In the end my feeling so bad was nothing to do with him.'

He lifted his hand and cupped her cheek.

'I didn't realise it at first, but *you'd* already filled that gap—with light and laughter. I want that back. I want to be with you. Because when you were gone… When I'd lost you…'

She curled her hands into fists. So tense. So terrified. 'I don't want to be dependent on you…'

'You trust Tara…you let your other friends help you… why not me?'

'I don't feel the same way about them as I do you,' she whispered.

'I'm kinda glad about that,' he whispered back. 'So how *do* you feel about me?'

'It's so intense it's terrifying,' she admitted. 'One look from you and I'm ready to—'

'To what?'

'Follow you to all four corners of the earth… One touch from you and I'm willing to cast off all my plans and do whatever you want me to.' She crumpled. 'I don't want to drown in this…and I already have. I left my brother in the lurch for two days straight—'

'And you arranged for Tara to check up on him that whole time,' Jack pointed out, holding her close.

'It can't be healthy…' She frowned, wishing he could understand. 'I can't do that. I can't be like my mum—giving everything up for a guy.'

'But I'll *never* ask you to give up everything. I'd never ask you to leave Dan. Your blog. Your life. But it can't be right to ignore what's between us either. To walk away from something that could be so fantastic.'

He held her shoulders and looked into her face.

'I've seen great love, Stephanie. My adoptive parents—they know how to love. And we have to give this a chance. We can work it out. We have to try. We're both worth that. We could be everything. *Have* everything. Don't you see?'

He gazed at her with those gorgeous, intense eyes.

'I never knew how lonely I was until I had you. Then lost you.' He stood, framing her face between his two strong hands. 'Trust me. Trust yourself.' He swallowed. 'Are you willing to try?'

Her heart beat so fast. But she already knew the answer. She'd known it before he'd even knocked on her door. Because she'd already learned from him—and from Dan—that she couldn't be a coward any more.

No matter how scared she was.

'Yes.'

He swept her into his arms, kissing her with all the pent-up passion of three days' absence.

She reached up and clung to him. 'How is this ever going to work?'

'I'll stay here,' he answered readily. 'I like Australia.'

She shook her head. 'I don't want to trap you here. Maybe we could compromise?'

'Spend some time everywhere?' He smiled as she nodded. 'Do you want to make a list?' he teased. 'All the places you want to go?'

'Actually…' She sent him a look. 'Right now I want to make a list of all the things I want to *do*.'

'Got a pen handy?'

'I don't need a pen.' She reached up on tiptoe and cooed at him—ultra-Steffi Leigh. 'I'm going to write the list with my tongue.'

'Huh?' He pressed her closer. 'Where are you going to write this list?'

'Over every inch of your body.'

'It's a big list?'

'*Very* big.'

She caught his eye and laughed. But then he kissed her again and everything changed. All the heartache and insecurity and loss of the last few days surged. She gripped him close and gave herself over to his care—kissing and kissing and *giving*.

He held her so deliciously tightly she could hardly breathe. It didn't matter. Being in his arms was the only way to go.

Slowly the desperation in their kisses eased, then morphed from assuaging pain to celebrating pure happiness…to driving sensual need.

'I need to *be* with you,' she begged. Utterly honest. Utterly undone. 'I need you inside me.'

But he stepped back, turning to pull her down to the old sofa with him.

'I have a list of my own, you know.' He chuckled, that old wicked, provocative look in his eyes.

'You do?' Her damn toes curled at that look of his.

'Thought it up on it on the flight over: "Ten Ways to Make Steffi Leigh Scream". Want me to spell them out for you?'

'Do I *want*?' she repeated. Then she reached out and pulled on his tee shirt, falling backwards so he fell on top of her. *'Duh…'*

# EPILOGUE

*One year later*

JACK SMILED AT the matron as they said their goodbyes, and then put his arm around Stephanie's waist to lead her to the waiting car.

His girlfriend had been unusually silent as they'd toured the orphanage. He'd seen her sweet heart in her eyes—aching as she'd looked around the facility. He knew she'd barely held it together when they'd spent time with the children—some of whom he saw year after year—and he'd read one of the books he'd brought with him to add to their library.

She'd chosen some children's art books as well, and they'd donated craft supplies.

'You want to take them all home, don't you?' He melted inside as he saw the tears in her eyes as their taxi pulled away from the building.

She nodded. 'It doesn't seem right to be going back to that hotel…'

'It's okay…' He cradled her against his side as the car pulled away.

'How do you do it?' She wiped a tear from her cheek.

'I'm trying to help…that's the one thing I *can* do.' He shrugged. 'That's why I keep coming back.'

That was why the orphanage was where so much of his charity funding was directed.

She nodded, but was quiet as she exited the car. He

couldn't wait to hold her properly, to love her properly. But for that they needed to be alone.

He held her hand as they rode up the elevator to their hotel room. And then, thank goodness, they were there.

She turned to face him as soon as she'd stepped inside the room, reached up to hug him. He loved it that she reached out when she needed him now. That she let him comfort her.

'Do you think we could take *one* of them home?' she asked softly, her face pressed against his chest.

He wrapped both arms around her and held her closer. 'You want to adopt?'

'If it would help one of those guys, then, yes—of course I do,' she said. 'But I'm so conscious of taking someone away from their home country.'

'I've taken you from yours.'

She'd gone with him to the States. Travelled with him. Updated her blog from wherever she was. She didn't need to rely on her friends to supply her with data for her lists as much any more.

She chuckled, 'We go back there all the time!'

That was true. They'd agreed to spend half the year in or near Australia—so she and Dan would be as close as ever, but getting on with their own lives.

'I want to come back *here* all the time too,' she said, lifting her head to look him in the eyes. 'I want to help the way you do.'

His heart pounded as he saw the love in her face. He wanted her. *So* much. The desire was so intense it hurt. Even now, when they'd been together a year already, that passion hadn't abated. If anything it was more potent. And he saw the signs of it within her too—the dilation of her pupils, the extra-strong gleam of green, the slight breathlessness, the colour in her cheeks despite that pretty layer of make-up. And then there was the way her nipples poked through her silken dress. On this hot, hot day it was arousal lifting those goosebumps on her skin.

But there was something else he'd been wanting for a while now.

'Maybe we ought to get married first,' he said huskily. 'Before we start adding kids to the mix.'

She stared up at him, her soulful eyes widening even more.

He reached into his pocket, pulled out the box that had been weighing him down for the last few days while he waited for the right moment. This was definitely the right moment.

He hoped.

He flicked open the box and showed her the contents. He'd seen it a million times already—from concept to design to completion. The square-cut diamond was, he hoped, perfect for her.

But she'd gone very, very quiet. Her beautiful eyes had filled with tears again.

He licked his lips and decided the tears were a *good* sign.

'I figure it's like a brick,' he said, going fully old-fashioned and dropping to his knee. He lifted the ring from the box and caught her hand.

'You said it!' She choked on a teary laugh.

'It's supposed to symbolise a foundation stone. When we first met I was wanting to know about my past. But then I learned that what really matters is building my future. So I'm building the future I want. With *you*.' He looked up at her. 'Will you accept it? Will you marry me?'

'Oh, yes.' She threw her arms around his neck, bending to kiss him. 'I love you, Jack Wolfe.'

'I love *you*, Stephanie Johnson. Every beautiful bit of you.' He stood and drew her into his arms. 'I'm *always* going to love you.'

\* \* \*

An hour later Stephanie rolled onto her back and picked up her phone. Getting the right angle, she snapped a picture of the gorgeous ring on her finger.

'For the blog?' Jack asked lazily beside her.

'No!' She laughed. 'For my brother.'

Her blog was still in existence, though she didn't update it as often. She'd abandoned any idea of monetising it—now it was purely for fun. She didn't feel the pressure to post every other day for fear of losing all her followers, and it was bliss. She'd convinced Tara to step up more formally, as she deserved, so now there were two names in the tagline.

She and Jack had spent half the year in Australia, half in the States, and had travelled extensively all the time. She'd written some pieces for the Wolfe Guides, and taken photos for the website he'd got his designers to develop.

Now she smiled as a series of texts pinged back from her brother. He'd gone crazy with the emoticons—and they brought stupidly happy tears to her eyes.

*Too many tears, already.*

'He wants to meet us in New York for Christmas,' she told Jack as she read the messages. 'He's looking forward to the flight.'

'That's fantastic.'

'Yeah.'

Dan was in full-time study and working towards his goal of becoming a teacher. And he reckoned he was training as well—aiming for the stars already, right back to super-sportsman.

'Put your phone down, "Steffi Leigh", and come pay attention to me.'

She tossed her phone to the floor and rolled back towards her handsome fiancé. 'Face to face?'

'Yes, please,' he muttered, sliding his hand down her back to pull her right on top of him. 'In real life.'

'*Very* real,' she murmured as she kissed him.

'You have no idea how much I love you.'

'Yes, I do.' She slid over him, feeling him touch her deeply—physically, emotionally. 'With all your heart. And it's such a big heart.'

'Overflowing right now,' he groaned.

'I'll take it,' she whispered, just before she kissed him again. 'I'll take it all. And I'll give you everything I can in return.'

'Fairy princess…' He smiled at her. 'You already have.'

* * * * *